I0762307

Remember The Poor And The Needy Among Us

Grace Dola Balogun

Grace Religious Books Publishing & Distributors, Inc. New York

Hardcover ISBN: 9781939415547
Softcover ISBN: 9781939415530
Library of Congress Control Number: 2013956553

Published by:
Grace Religious Books Publishing & Distributors, Inc.
213 Bennett Avenue New York, NY, 10040

Cover design by Lisa Hainline www.lisahainline.com
Printed in the United States of America www.gracereligiousbookspublishers.com

It turns out that advancing equal opportunity and economic empowerment is both morally right and good economics, because discrimination, poverty and ignorance restrict growth, while investments in education, infrastructure and scientific and technological research increase it, creating more good jobs and new wealth for all of us.

—William J. Clinton

CONTENTS

I want to wage war against illiteracy, poverty, unemployment, unfair competition, communitarianism, delinquency.

—Nicolas Sarkozy

DEDICATION

I dedicate this book to God the Father, God the Son and God the Holy Spirit. The Father so loved the world that he gave his only begotten Son that those who believe in him will not perish but have eternal life, life everlasting. I thank God the Father Almighty for his indescribable, unspeakable, incomparable gift of our Lord of lords, Our Lord and Savior Jesus Christ, the King of kings, the only begotten Son of God born unto this earth.

Christ gave himself for the people of this world for atoning sacrifice for our past, present and future sins. He is the only one who is worthy of our praises and adoration. He said, "The poor you will always have with you, but you will not always have me" (Matthew 26:11). In the Old Testament, he commanded the Israelites to remember the poor and care for them. He is the God of the poor and the needy, the afflicted, the sick, the disabled, the distressed and the people suffering in various ways.

I also dedicate this book to all who will read it and find life in Jesus Christ the Lord of lords and the light of this world, the true light that shines forever and no darkness can comprehend it. Those who will read the book and acquire a great knowledge of Scripture that will make them wise and live a life approved by God, they will know clearly that God did want us to remember the poor among us and help them. Reading this book will make the rich countries make every effort to help the poor people in their country. It will help the rich people to develop a good helping relationship with the poor. It will also let the poor people know that God did not forget about them. Reading this book will help the reader to gain the knowledge of how God is still calling you and me and speaks to his people today telling them to give cheerfully, not sparingly to the charitable organizations that care for the needy. If God blesses you abundantly today please remember the poor, the afflicted, distressed and disabled, and know that the same God is concerned for the rich and the poor. There is no difference in the eyes of God.

I was a very poor young black boy in New Orleans, just a face without a name, swimming in a sea of poverty trying to survive.

—Tyler Perry

PREFACE

"He defends the cause of the fatherless and widow, and loves the alien, giving him food and clothing." "At the end of every three years, bring all the tithes of that year's produce and store it in your lawns, so that the Levites who have no allotment or inheritance of their own and the aliens, the fathers and the widows who live in your towns may come and eat and be satisfied, so that the Lord your God may bless you in all the work of your hands" (Deuteronomy 10:18, 14:28-29). Sp that he Lord God continues and said, "If there is a poor man among your brothers in any of the towns of the land that the Lord your God is giving you do not be hardhearted or tightfisted toward your poor brother. Rather be openhanded and freely lend him whatever he needs." (Deuteronomy 15:7-8).

God wants us to be good to the poor people, as there will always be poor among the people in the world. God commanded that Christians should give according to their ability and according to how necessary and important the needs of the poor are. Christians must not harden their heart to the needy and the poor. When there is an occasion of charitable lending or giving, if we cannot trust the needy or the borrower we must trust God, hoping for nothing. If they pay it back fine; if they do not pay it back, you know that you did it for the Lord, and expecting that you will be recompensed in the resurrection of the just. Our Lord said, "Love your enemies and do good to them" (Luke 6:35).

Our Lord and Savior Jesus Christ commanded this difficult duty to his followers; it is represented as a generous thing to do. To love those who loved us it very simple, but to love those who hate us, love our enemies. It's the most difficult thing to do, but our Lord said we must do it in order to be like him.

Christian believers must make it their duty to honor God and love him forever; we must love our neighbors and we must love ourselves. Fear the

Lord as a great God, and Lord. Love him as a good God and as our heavenly Father. All Christians must be ready to serve the Lord with all their soul and hearts, cheerfully and with joy. Keep his commandments at all times; love the strangers around them.

God's providence, which extends from one corner of the earth to another, never fails, because we are made of one blood. He gave to all life and breathes all things to both gentiles and Israelites. Those Christians who have not gone through afflictions and trials must have feelings toward those who are being afflicted, those who are in distress and show them a great kindness.

Christians must give part of what God provides for them to increase the work of the Lord on this earth. The tithe stands as maintenance. It must be set apart for God. They must also give their resources to charity—to the poor, so that the poor may have something to eat and be satisfied. The Scripture said, "And you will be blessed. Although they cannot repay you, you will be repaid at the resurrection of the righteous" (Luke 14:14). When you make a feat, invite the poor and the maimed. People who have nothing to live upon and the people that were unable to work for a living, feeding them clothing them, these types of charity are the true charity because they cannot pay you back, but they will pay you back with their prayers. This type of charity may not be rewarded on this earth, but they will not lose their rewards.

Scripture revealed again and again that God always concerned about the poor and all poverty that is going on in the world. In so many ways, God provides for the poor. The Lord God Almighty defends the fathers, the orphans in the orphanage homes and the widows. He commanded in the Old Testament that they should give them food as well as they must clothe them. He also instituted the system of tithes every three year from the people who work and have plenty of money to pay tithes. Therefore, out of the tithes that people paid, God will use part of it to feed, clothe and care for those who are in need, especially the widows who have no children and no husband.

The Lord God Almighty also used part of the tithe to shelter the homeless, the fatherless and the sick. The Lord is telling us not to be too hard on any of our brothers who are poor. We should not be hardhearted or tightfisted toward them. God wants us to be openhanded and cheerfully, freely help the poor among us while he promised to help us and bless us. The more we open our hand to help the needy, the more the Lord rushes his blessings upon us without measure. Let us earnestly and joyfully help the poor among us. Let the word of God dwell richly in our heart so that we can be able to serve God acceptably and sincerely in all the areas of our lives.

My attitude to peace is rather based on the Burmese definition of peace— it really means removing all the negative factors that destroy peace in this world. So, peace does not mean just putting an end to violence or to war, but to all other factors that threaten peace, such as discrimination, such as inequality, poverty.

—Aung San Suu Kyi

"Three times a year all your men must appear before the Lord your God at the place he will choose at the Feast of Unleavened Bread, the Feast of Weeks and the Feast Tabernacles. No man Should appear before the Lord empty-handed"

(Deuteronomy 16:16)

CHAPTER ONE
Biblical Interpretation Of Poverty

People of this earth must be obedient to God's law in order to grow out of a sincere desire to help those who are in need. God cares about our attitude and our desire to help the poor, the needy and the people who are unfortunate. We must use all that we have including our material possessions to help those who have real needs. "Do not take advantage of a hired man who is poor and needy, whether he is a brother Israelite or an alien living in one of your towns. Pay him his wages each day before Sun set, because he is poor and is counting on it. Otherwise he may cry to the Lord against you, and you will be guilty of sin" (Deuteronomy 24:14-15). Our Lord commanded that those who have servants must be just to them and treat them fairly. They must not oppress them. God wants the masters to be faithful to their servants and pay them their wages on time.

Those who are working from day to day must be paid, as they live from hand to mouth every day. They might not have food for their family if they are not paid for their daily work. Magistrates and judges are commanded by the Lord to be just in their duties. The rich are commanded to be kind and to be charitable to the poor. In many ways, the Lord commanded the rich to take care of the poor among them. They should allow the poor to pick up the left over corn, grapes and olive oil. They should leave plenty behind so that the poor will have enough to eat. God warned the nation of Israel in the Old Testament that they must not take advantage of the poor among them, but to treat them with compassion and with respect. Christian believers who fail to treat the poor and the needy fairly will bring to themselves God's condemnation.

Poverty in the Scripture can be characterized as both social and spiritual. Poverty is a very sensitive and delicate issue that affects all people all over the face of the earth. "And do not show favoritism to a poor man in his lawsuit" (Exodus 23:3). As part of the covenant, a poor person must be treated with respect and they must be supported economically. People of Israel who are rich must not charge interest to the poor people. In direct legislation, a member of institutions contained special provisions for poor people. Gleaning laws are laws that provide for the poor. Gleaning focused on the widows who have no one to care for them; the fatherless, strangers and poor. In the Old Testament, Jubilee provided release for the people who had become servants through poverty. Jubilee festivals provide free food produced of all the grains in the fields that the poor people could also be able to eat freely.

Another help for the poor is that the poor were included in the right of redemption from slavery by a blood relative, supported from their third year tithe. "If an alien, temporary resident among you become rich and one of your countrymen becomes poor and sells himself to the alien living among you or a member of the alien's clan, he retains the right of his relatives in his clan may redeem him. Or if he prospers, he may redeem himself. He and his buyer are to count the time from the year he sold himself up to the year of Jubilee" (Leviticus 25:47-50). "Worship the Lord your God, and his blessings will be on your food and water. I will take away sickness from among you, and no one will miscarry or be barren in your land. I will give you a full life span" (Exodus 23:25-26). God connected the removal of sickness from among his people when they have wholehearted devotion to him and they were separated from the ungodly influences around them.

God the Father made a law called the Law of Moses that the poor must be relieved. Our brothers and sisters, those who are in poverty and distress, their problems must be our problem. All the people of this world must look upon others and treat each other as brothers and sisters. We must see that we all have the same Father. By sympathy, pitying the poor, by service we must do them good; by supplying; supply them all that they need according to their necessity and ability.

The scripture revealed that those who help the poor are the righteous people. Always help the poor while the wicked will laugh at them and they will not help them. From time to time, God called his people and the church to help the poor people in our society. This action is the model of Jesus Christ and the word of God. This action is also the very nature of God. The Scripture said, "For God so love the world he gave his only Son" (John 3:16). This is the greatest gospel mystery that was revealed to mankind. "For God loved the world that he gave his only begotten son." Jesus Christ is the only begotten Son of God. God the Father showed his love to us when he gave his only begotten Son to the world. God gave him to us to suffer for us. His enemies could not have overpowered him if the Father did not permit it or given him to them. Jewish people believed that the Messiah is only for the nation of Israel, but Christ told them that he came in love to the people in the whole world. Through Christ, we have a general offer of the Life of salvation made to all human beings. Jesus Christ came to this world with salvation in his hand and in his eyes. Christ did not condemn the world. He wants everyone in the world to have the gift of grace and salvation.

The love of God for all the inhabitants of the earth is incomparable and incomprehensible. Our world is full of two categories of people those who are rich and those who are poor, which means some people have plenty wherever they may be on this earth. Some have not. Those who have always used and taken advantage of those who have not, such as paying lower wages than they should pay, telling them to do illegal business for them, take a fund raising without giving the money raised to the people they raised the money for; they used the money for their own gain and lust. In most cases, the rich always exploit the poor. The Scripture revealed how God sent his messenger prophet Amos to the people of Israel and he continues to send messages to us today.

"For I know how many are your offenses and how great your sins. You oppress the righteous and take bribes and you deprive the poor of justice in the courts. Therefore, the prudent man keeps quiet in such times, for the times are evil. Seek good, not evil, that you may live. Then the Lord God Almighty will be with you, just as you say he is" (Amos 5:12-14). The rich people in the Old Testament turned the law against those who were innocent, those who departed from evil and those who lived a quiet life on the land. They were bribed by the rich in order to patronize and protect themselves and they oppressed the poor. They sent away the poor from their gate in the court's justice. They were very malicious and they were the prosecutors of God's faithful children, God's servants. Ministers and prophets gave the word and the message of God. God himself told them that when the fire of his judgments should kindle upon them all the gods they served would not be able to save them.

Out of all the sins that prophet Amos pointed out, the most prominent sins were the people's social sins. The rich are taking advantage of the poor and continually exploiting them. It is God's will that we Christians should have a special love and compassion for the needy. The power of the Holy Spirit indwelling helps Christians to help the poor. "The Lord sends poverty and wealth; he humbles and exalts. He raises the poor from the dust and lifts the needy from the ash heap; he seats them with princes and has them inherit a throne of honor, for the foundations of the earth are the Lord's upon them he has set the world" (1st Samuel 2:7-8).

Scripture revealed that Hannah prayed in the temple. God answered her prayers. Hannah possessed the spirit of prayers and the spirit of prophecy.

She received mercy from God with thankfulness and praise. Praise is our tribute; we are unjust if we do not praise our God. The mercy that Hanna received was an answer to prayer, and therefore, she thought herself to give thanks, for it. God is the sovereign Lord of life and death.

"The Lord killed and made alive," nothing is too hard or impossible for God to do. He quickening the dead and put life into dry bones. The Lord brings some low and lifts up others. He humbles the proud and gives grace and honor to the lowly. God lifts up those with his salvation who humble themselves before him. God the Father Almighty comforted and blessed Joseph, Daniel, Moses and David from prisons, great afflictions and moved them to the palace from a sheep-hook to a scepter. God Almighty wants everyone who has plenty to remember those all around the world who do not have beginning with our neighborhood to the end of the world.

Christians must remember the poor and those who are sick among us to pray for them and care for their needs. The Scripture revealed, in the book of Job, "Like wild donkeys in the desert, the poor go about their labor of foraging food; the waste land provides food for their children" (Job 24:5). The rich loved in their heart. Out of their hearts they brag over poor people and they turned them away from getting relief; they also threatened them and forced them to abscond. Especially the poor children that were fatherless, they also made them motherless after they took away their father's life. They broke the mother's heart, and starved the children and left them to die. People like this forget about the judgment of God; they show no mercy to the poor and they shall not receive mercy from God.

God always takes care, plans and sustains the poor among us. God did not say remember the rich, but he said remember the poor among you and do them good. A poor man is the image of Jesus Christ; all Christians are the image of the Lord Jesus, for he sacrifices our influence of Christ and makes them like Jesus Christ. They love what Christ loves and hate what Christ hates.

The poor are like their masters not only in behavioral and moral issues, and character but also in all circumstances of life. People of this world can see Christ clearly in the believing Christians, but they cannot see, or it is very hard to see, Christ in the rich people because they tend to puff up and are full of pride as well as arrogant, and show off that they are the one, not God, doing things through them.

God is always concerned for the fatherless, the widow, the orphan and the people who are called refugees having problems in their country and becoming refugees in another country. God the Father Almighty wants us to help them, especially those who are disadvantaged. God will be well pleased if we help them in the time of their difficulties. The Scripture revealed in the book of Proverbs, "He who despises his neighbor sins, but blessed is he who is kind to the needy" (Proverbs 14:21). The Scripture tells us that whoever does wrong to the poor will answer to his maker. God makes the poor and the needy and gives them life as he gave to the rich; both the rich and the poor have one Father and one maker. The poor honored what was done to them, but will show themselves pleased for the kindness that was shown to them. Please them accordingly.

The Scripture teaches all the Christian believers how to care for and treat the poor. From time to time, God almighty in various ways and in every area of our lives, expressed his great concern for the poor, the needy, oppressed, afflicted, fatherless, widows, orphaned and the lonely people in the world.

The Scripture revealed, "You evildoers frustrate the plans of the poor, but the Lord is their refuge" "In his arrogance the wicked man hunts down the weak, who are caught in the schemes he devises" (Psalm 14:6, 10:2). When David was going through a lot of problems and he was driven out by Absalom and his rebellious people, he was comforted with the word of assurance that God will deliver him from the hands of his enemies. David knew that God's salvation would one day come and would help the poor in their state of poverty.

The wicked are very proud and they continually persecute the poor. In this Scripture, the psalmist prays that God will overthrow the wicked people, help the helpless and reign as King forever in order that sin and evil and terror might be abolished from the world. The Lord is the refuge, the helper, the provider and the deliverer of the poor from generation to generation. What God Almighty revealed is covenant law to the people of Israel; he provides so many ways for them to make sure that poverty is abolished completely among them.

"Giving generously to him and do so without a grudging heart; then because of this the Lord your God will bless you in all your work and in everything you put your hand to. There will always be poor people in the land. Therefore, I command you to be open handed toward your brothers and towards the poor and the needy in your land" (Deuteronomy 15:10-11). Christians must not have a spirit of greediness or selfishness. The spirit that does not care for the poor that ignores the needs of other people around him or her; a spirit like this deprives Christians from the measure of the blessings of the Lord.

The new life in Jesus Christ emphasizes that Christians must have compassion, empathy, kindness and love for those who have suffered various kinds of setbacks and experience unfortunate circumstances that cause poverty and various needs. According to the Scripture "However, there should be no poor among you, for in the land the Lord your God is giving you to possess as your inheritance, he will richly bless you, if only you fully obey the Lord your God and are careful to follow all these commands I am giving you today. For the Lord your God will bless you as he has promised, and you will lend to many nations but will borrow from none. You will rule over many nations but none will rule over you" (Deuteronomy 15:4-6).

God also forbade the charging of interest on loans to the poor, "If one of your country men becomes poor and is unable to support himself among you, help him as you would an alien or a temporarily resident, so he can continue to live among you. Do not take interest of any kind from him, but fear God, so that your countryman may continue to live among you. You must not lend him money at interest or sell him food at a profit" (Leviticus 25:35-37). "These are the regulations for the woman who gives birth to a boy or a girl. If when cannot afford a Lamb, she is to bring two doves or two young pigeons, one for a burnt offering and the other for a sin offering. In this way the priest will make atonement for her, and she will be clean" (Leviticus 12: 7b-8). The sin offering is for the rich and the poor. Whatever difference there may be between the rich and the poor in the sacrifice of acknowledgement, atonement is the same for both the rich and the poor. This sin offering was intended either to complete people's purification from ceremonial uncleanness, which though it was not in itself sinful, it was typically of human moral pollution, or to make an atonement for that which was really sin.

God in his mercy wants people of this earth to help each other—especially Christian believers—God prohibited the charging of interest for loans to the needy to supply their basic needs. God always protected the poor from the exploitation of the rich. These laws, however, do not apply to the middle class. Israelites who need money to establish their business may have interest on business loans or many loans for commercial purposes.

We can see clearly how God became involved in all areas of our lives with his love. The Lord also said that during the harvest season the grain that dropped was to be left so that the poor people could pick it up for food. God also commanded that the edges of the harvest field must be left unharvested for the picking for the poor. God also commanded that every seventh year whoever owed money for seven years and was unable to pay, the debt must be canceled. In addition, those who have money must not refuse to loan it to those who do not have money. Unfortunately, the Israelites do not always keep this Law of God; instead, many rich Israelites took advantage of the poor and increased their problems. The same is true today. If anyone owed money for seven years the debt is automatically canceled from the collection agency.

Lord God Almighty sent prophet Amos to them about the judgment against the wealthy, and the rich in Israel and the rich people today. In the New Testament, God also exercised a deep concern for the poor, the needy and the oppressed, especially those poor in the Christian church. Jesus Christ's ministry also concerns the poor and the disadvantaged during his earthly ministry. Christ cared about the people who no one cared for, such as people who were oppressed and afflicted, the sick, the lepers, the disabled and the blind.

Jesus Christ spoke to those who clung to all the material things and worldly things of these world possessions and ignored the afflicted, those who do not care for the poor and the needy. Our Lord Jesus Christ wants all Christians to care for the poor and give generously for the care of the sick and people with various needs. "Be careful not to do your acts of righteousness before men, to be seen by them. If you do, you will have no reward from your Father in heaven. Therefore, when you give to the needy, do not announce it with trumpets, as the hypocrites do in the synagogues and on the streets, to be honored by men. I tell you the truth they have received their reward in full" (Matthew 6:1-20). Our Lord said; when you give alms do not let your left hand know what your right hand did to the poor. Let not your left hand knows; Christians must conceal it as much as possible. They must keep it in private because it is good work done for the Lord. To avoid pride that can come out of it by the reaction of the people around us, people and Christians should make their alms secret; God, who sees in secret, will reward them openly. God is our Father who gives abundantly more than what we cannot imagine to his children who deserve it.

When Mary was putting the oil on Christ's feet, wiping them with tears and her hair, Judas Iscariot thought that it was a waste but it was the highest respect and love for Jesus Christ, the Messiah, the holy child of Bethlehem. Where there is time to love, we must put the best behavior upon everything that we do. There may be overdoing of our well doing but we must learn not to be censorious of other people around us because we may impute prudence. God may accept it as an instance of abundant love. The same is true today: Christ Jesus loves those who give out of kindness of their heart to show their appreciation of the good thing someone did for them, not only to the poor and the needy, the appreciation, acknowledgment of other people toward us.

The principle here condemns our motives for acting righteously. If any Christians, whether ministers, or pastors, elders or deacons in the church, do good for the administration of others, or for selfish reasons, they will lose their reward and praise from God. Instead, they will stand exposed as hypocrites who, under the guise of giving glory to God, are really seeking glory for themselves. Christ teaches about the acts of righteousness and giving in three important areas: (1) prayer—Jesus wants us to pray for all our needs. Fasting and prayers help us to be spiritually grown in the Lord. Christ condemned the act of righteousness to be seen by others, competing about who gives more to the church, or who are performing and entertaining more people in the church, and wanting to be the first. Apostle Paul and Apostle Peter and the early church likewise, demonstrated deep concern for those who are in need among them. The Scripture revealed, "One of them named Agabus stood up and through the spirit predicted that a severe famine would spread over the entire Roman world. This happened during the reign of Claudius. The disciples, each according to his ability, decided to provide help for the brothers living in Judea. This they did, sending their gift to the elders by Barnabas and Saul" (Act 11:28-29). In the first council meeting in Jerusalem, the elders and leaders who debate about circumcision or no circumcision, strictly warn Barnabas and Paul that they must remember the poor. One of the goals of Apostle Paul is to help the poor. A Christians' first priority must be the care of the needy in the church of Jesus Christ. During the apostle era, a man called Agabus prophesied about famine that was approaching the nation. He also stood up and prophesied, signified by the spirit, that there was going to be a famine and it could cause great death throughout the entire world. Many poor people would die because of the lack of food. The prophesy specified that famine would affect all the Roman Empire. This prophesy came to pass in the year of Claudius Caesar, which began in the second year of his reign and it was not ended until the fourth year but upon all the predictions people did not put away enough or hoard up corn for themselves as many Christians, which set up charity to relieve other people who were in need of food. Christians must have or exercise respect, or regard to all the household of faith who are in need of our help. Christians must not neglect the poor among them because God loves the poor as well as the rich.

God loves those who have and those who do not have. Communication between churches of Jesus Christ among the saints must be extended more and more in order to make provisions for those who are in need and for the relief of the poor in Judea who are there brothers. The apostles realized that the majority of those who converted to Christianity in Judea were the poor people. Therefore, if there is a famine it will affect the poor people very hard and they don't want them to perish for lack of food; which will be a great reproach to the Christian profession and their community. Because of this, they take care of the poor among them by making a provision for them before the famine began, or before it was too late to rescue them. The agreement pleased all the apostles. Every man contributed according to their ability to the good work of helping the poor. We should be doing the same thing today; Christians must care for each other and communicate with each other in the church in order to open up a channel of helping each other.

I have committed my life to helping the poor, and I believe that if more companies followed Wal-Mart's lead in providing opportunity and savings to those who need it most, more Americans battling poverty would realize the American dream.

—Andrew Young

CHAPTER TWO
"Christ Became Poor For Us"

"Because of the oppression of the weak and the groaning of the needy, I will now rise, says the Lord, I will protect them from those who malign them" (Psalm 12:5). God Almighty takes notice of the poor and the needy who were oppressed, abused and puffed. The poor have a God to go to because God will certainly help them and be a refuge to them. God, in an untimely and in an automatic way, works and delivers the poor oppressed people, shelters the homeless, clothes the naked, and feeds the poor hungry people who call unto him sincerely day and night.

God Almighty will keep all his children safe and protect them from evil people forever. Our Lord and Savior Jesus Christ was born of the Virgin Mary as a poor child in a manger at Bethlehem of Judea even though he is the eternal, which means he is before all things and in him all things consist in heaven and on earth.

Jesus Christ is the immortal, the invisible and the only wise God. He has no beginning and he has no end. Jesus Christ left all his glory in heaven and became poor in order to redeem us from all our sin; for the sake of humanity, he became poor. The Scripture revealed, "If I were hungry, I would not tell you for the world is mine, and all that is in it" (Psalm 50:12). God directed his people to be the best sacrifice of prayers and praise as those under the law, preferred before all the burnt offerings and sacrifices on which now under the gospel. What our Lord God requires from his people and what he will accept, we must acknowledge our sins, confess them and we must give God thanks, either poor or rich, for his mercies upon us.

God Almighty said that everything on this earth belongs to him. The hidden treasures of gold and the pearls that the diver cannot reach belong to him. He owns every precious thing that the earth has seen and has not seen. The Lord calls continually all Christian believers including all the people in this world. He invites all the faithful to call onto him in times of need and troubles. God desires to hear our prayers, to help us and to have his name exalted as a God who delivers his people. Christ has the power over all his creations. If he pleases, he could lay his hands on them; at his will, legions of angels will stand before him upon his command. He has the power to call riches to being at his command. Every wealth of the earth was at his command; he created them all.

Jesus Christ the creator of all things a newborn King in a cradle where the animals sleep in stables, in the manger rapped in swaddling clothes of children of poverty. He later became a stranger in the land of Egypt in order to be saved from the hand of King Herod. Christ has no comparison in terms of his poverty. He was poorer than any other men were; he was the King of poverty. Jesus Christ assisted his father when he was growing up in Nazareth as a carpenter. The creator of the Universe held hammer and nails working on boxes and tables with his father in a carpentry works.

Christ Jesus was in the lowest vale of poverty. His clothe was the garment of the poor. His food was from the people or from his friends or disciples. He sometimes depended upon charity from other people while preaching, teaching for the relief of his wants. At one point, Jesus Christ said, "Foxes have holes and birds of the air have nets, but the son of man has no place to lay his head" (Luke 9:58). Christ came to this world not to promise himself great things in the world; he said the son of man has not a place to lay his head. He became poor so that we could be rich; Christ took upon himself a very low condition when he was on earth. He did not delight himself in ornaments of gold, or diamond, but he delighted in a simple place to accommodate for mere necessity, as the foxes and the birds of the air. Jesus Christ, who made all things, did not make a dwelling place for himself, not a house of his own to put over his head. Christ calls himself Son of man, a Son of Adam, partaker of flesh and blood. Christ glories only in his condescension toward his disciples and us today, to testify his love for humanity, and he teaches us a holy contempt of the world, and a continual regard and respect to another world.

Christ was poor, to sanctify and sweeten poverty to his people. We Christians must follow Christ's part and be content in whatever state we are from one point to another in this world. All those who want to follow Christ must put this in consideration. Lie cold and uneasy, work hard, and live in pretend to follow Christ. Christ tells the man what he must count upon if he is ready to follow him.

Jesus Christ had nowhere to lay his head. He became the servant of the servants by taking a towel and washing his disciples' feet after he girded himself.

Jesus Christ our Savior, during his earthly ministry, said in plain language that he had no place to live or sleep while in this world; Christ had no place that he could call his own. These words of Jesus Christ were prophesied in the Book of Revelation—Our Lord Jesus could have used other words to express his position during his earthly look of abiding place, a room for himself, or an apartment as we call it today. The Scripture revealed, "When evening came, many who were demon possessed were brought to him, and he drove out the spirits with a word and healed all the sick." This was to fulfill what was spoken through the prophet Isaiah, "He took up our infirmities and carried our diseases" (Matthew 8:16-17). When our Lord was in the world he cast out evil spirits by his word. This shows clearly that Christ have power over Satan. He headed all diversity of diseases and performed many, many miracles. This fulfilled prophet Isaiah's prophesy. Our sins make our sicknesses our grief. Christ carried away our sins by the merit of his death on the cross. He carried away our sickness by the miracle of his life. Christ carried our diseases, our shame. He comforted us. He carried our sins for us in his passion and carried them with us in his compassion. Christ, our Savior Lord, carried all our infirmities so that we may live and serve him forever.

Jesus Christ heals all those who are sick. God is the God of provisions, and protections God's purpose of redemption of our Lord Jesus Christ was before the foundation of the universe. His provision in redemption was extensive, the same as consequences of Adam and Eve fall. For sin, God Almighty provides forgiveness; God's provision for death is the eternal and resurrection life and for sickness, God provides healing. Jesus Christ's earthly ministry was based on these three things. Jesus Christ teaches God's word. He is the greatest teacher that the world has ever known.

Jesus Christ preached repentance of sins of all the people in the world and he explained the blessings of God's Kingdom, love and life of God from the earth to heaven. Thirdly, Jesus Christ healed all those who were sick, various sicknesses and diseases and carried all the infirmities of people. Jesus Christ, the true and as the incarnate Son of God, was and is the exact representation of God's nature, character and attributes during and throughout his earthly ministry.

"At this I fell at his feet to worship him but he said to me, do not do it I am a fellow servant with you and with your brothers who hold to the testimony of Jesus. Worship God, for the testimony of Jesus is the spirit of prophecy" (Revelation 19:10). This shows that, ultimately, all prophecy is related to Jesus and his redemptive work and is for his exaltation, in the gospel of God the Father and the Holy Spirit. Jesus Christ is a God loving servant. He takes a humble position of serving those who are sick, oppressed and helpless, in sin; helping them to know God, the realm of the love of God in their lives in the spiritual realms, Christ's devotion to God the Father is one hundred percent. All Christian believers must worship God the Father, God the Son and God the Holy Spirit and him alone. We should worship as the angel said to the apostle John that he is a fellow servant of the Lord like him, that Jesus Christ is the head of the church to the glory of God the Father amen. He is the one who is worthy of our worship, our praises and our adoration. Honor and glory belongs to him now and forever, amen.

The Scripture revealed in the book of Isaiah, "You are my witnesses, declares the Lord, and my servant whom I have chosen, so that you may know and believe me and understand that I am he, before me no god was formed, nor will there be one after me. I, even I, am the Lord, and apart from me there is no Savior" (Isaiah 43:10-11). God the Father Almighty made this word clear. In the book of Isaiah, the prophet is the Lord's servant. Jesus Christ takes the position of God's servant as well while on earth in order to be our Savior. God's witnesses are summoned to appear to give evidence for him; it was Jesus Christ himself who was referred to in this Scripture of Prophet Isaiah. All the prophets testified to Christ, and Christ himself is the great prophet. He appeared and pleaded as God's witness. Today, God's people are witnesses for him and they give a testimony of their experience concerning the power of the gift of grace. The Messiah himself is given to humanity to be a witness for him to people who have always been and who can continue to eternity. The Lord said we are his witness and he is God. Beside him there is no other God. He is self-existent and self-sufficient; he is the only one to fear, trust and worship. God existed before the creation of the universe, light and from eternity; he is God. Before any idol worshipers, or idolaters, God is from everlasting to everlasting. He is the great I am, the great Jehovah, who is, who was and who is to come—God has an infinite and infallible knowledge and wisdom. He has an infinite as well as irresistible power to save to the utmost those who believe in him. He is the omniscience, the omnipotence and omnipresent, the Holy One of Israel, the King of kings and the Lord of lords, the God of gods, the creator of the universe.

Our Lord and Savior illustrated that he did not consider a place to live as an important issue; what is more important to him is the service of teaching, preaching doing what is good for all of humanity in the world. "For you know the grace of our Lord Jesus Christ that though he was rich yet for your sakes he became poor, so that you through his poverty might become rich" (2nd Corinthians 8:9). Christians should love bountifully and expect a good return at the end of their life on earth. The labor of love must be done like any other good works with thought and design freely given to the poor. Christians should give cheerfully not grudgingly or of necessity. They must know that when they give to the poor and the needy, they should never count it as lost; it is a precious seed, which is cast into the ground, is not lost, but it will spring up and bear fruit, more fruit to the kingdom of our Lord and Savior. The sower will receive it again with immeasurable increase—God loved a cheerful giver. People and Christians can never be losers if they are doing what is pleasing in the sight of the Lord. God will make our love abound to our advantage; Christian believer must trust in the goodness of our Lord; he is able to make all grace abound, honor, and the reward of eternal life.

We can see clearly that sacrificial giving was an essential part of Christ's nature and character. By his becoming poor, we now partakes of his eternal riches. God the Father expects the same attitude and character among the believing Christians and among the people of the entire world, as evinced by his grace working within his children.

All the gifts of grace and salvation, the Kingdom of heaven, and even disgrace, shame for the sake of Christ, are the everlasting riches we have received in exchange for the rags of sin. Jesus Christ became poor, that all the people on earth through his poverty might become rich in him; this is the poverty and wealth spiritually, which indicates the work of the Holy Spirit in our lives, as well as in the lives of all believers of Jesus Christ. Christ became poor for our sake. He had everything when he was rich in power, when he was omnipotence—all-powerful, he had everything at his command and he could do all things in the world but he became poor for the entire human race. He laid his glory aside and his power aside as he walked here on earth.

Jesus said, "Don't you believe that I am in the Father, and the Father is in me? The words I say to you are not just my own, rather, it is the Father, living in me, who is doing his work" (John 14:10). Jesus Christ is explaining to the people that he and the Father are one. Christ is in the Father, and the Father in Christ. Seeing Christ you have seen the Father. Jesus Christ is one with the Father. Knowing Christ, we know the Father. Christ said that the words that I speak are not from him; the Father spoke through him. The Father dwelled in Christ; in Christ, the Father may be found. Just as Christ is dwelling in all believers today, Christ lived his life through individual Christians. Jesus Christ's miracles are the proof of his divine missions to the world. Christ does his work through believing Christians just as the Father did his work through Christ during his earthly ministry.

Our Lord's desire is that all Christian believers should work as he worked while on earth. Christians must do the work of converting souls of people to Christ as well as performing miracles. Christians doing things for the Lord and the miracle of doing greater things for the Lord. Christ surrendered the use of his power and mind to the Father and to his Father's will. The Father took total control. What happened is that the son carried out the Father's plan.

The Father dwelled in him and did all the work, as Christ dwells in all the believing Christian and does all the work through us. When Christ was in heaven all the Seraphs and all the angels in heaven bowed down before him saying, "Holy, Holy, Holy is the Lord almighty, the whole earth is full of his glory" (Isaiah 6:3-6). This shows that God's absolute holiness must be proclaimed in the churches as it is proclaimed in the heavens. God Almighty must be praised; as the Lord of hosts of all hosts, one of his most respectable glorious attributes is his holiness. God's power on all his creations, his power was mentioned two times, but his holiness was mentioned three times always, Holy, Holy, Holy, which also referred to the three Godhead—God the Father, God the Son, God the Holy Spirit forever one God. The Lord, full of purity and power, is holy in all his ways; no one before him, no one after in heaven and in earth below, when he spoke people trembled and the earth shook at his words. God dwells in the light; there is no darkness in Him.

Christ became poor. Prophet Isaiah wrote, "He was despised and rejected by men, a man of sorrows, and familiar with suffering, like one from whom men hide their faces, he was despised, and we esteemed him not. Surely, he took up our infirmities and carried our sorrows. Yet we considered him stricken by God, smitten by him, and afflicted" (Isaiah 53:3-4). Jesus Christ in the book of Isaiah was described as a man of sorrows, despised and rejected. He was not settled in one place to call his own. He had nowhere to lay his head. He lived upon donations, the alms that people gave him when he taught or preached. Jesus Christ is a man of tender spirit. He admitted that sorrows and grief were his intimate acquaintance, for he acquainted himself with the grief of others. He sympathized with what people in this world are going through. Jesus Christ always has the beauty of his holiness, his goodness. He is the desire of all nations. "He was oppressed and afflicted, yet he open not his mouth" (Isaiah 53:7). He did not plead his own innocence. He freely offered himself as a lamb of sacrifice. He suffered and died for the sins of the people in the world on the cross. He voluntarily submitted to the suffering for great and holy ends by his own soul, his own life, an offering for the sin of humanity. It was because of our sins that Christ suffered on our behalf. His poverty makes us rich.

Instead of Christ being accepted by the people of Israel, he was hated and rejected by its rulers; Jesus' ministry, because of his rejection suffered great pain, anguish, disappointment and grief because of the sins of the human race. The same way all Christians will suffer and experience what Jesus Christ experienced, which is a measure of suffering and rejection from those you love. When Christ was rich in resources, everything was at his command because the Bible says of him and through him and to him are all things. In him we move; we have our being. Our Lord became poor. He said, "Son of man have no place to lay his head." Jesus Christ had no house. When he was born his mother and his earthly father borrowed a manger where he could be born; he borrowed a penny when he wanted to perform a miracle. He received help from others for his clothing. He went all over Judea, Samaria and Jerusalem preaching, teaching the gospel of God with no special dwelling place. Nothing was his own on this earth. The Scripture said, "then everyone deserted him and fled" (Mark 14:50). They all forsook him and fled. The apostles of Jesus Christ, Christ's disciples, deserted him. At first, they were very confident that they would never leave him that they would continue with him, and stood by him, but they all fled. We could imagine what that would cause to our Lord and Savior at that time and hour that they deserted him. It is going on today as well, how family and friends stay away, deserted believing Christians during the time of their suffering and affliction.

Jesus Christ borrowed a boat to preach. He borrowed a house for Passover. He borrowed a colt for triumphant entry to Jerusalem; "Lowly and riding on a donkey, a colt, the foal of a donkey," and a week before his crucifixion, he borrowed bread from a little boy to perform a miracle of feeding five thousand men not including women and children (Mark 6:32-44). Traveling by water is less troublesome than traveling by land. When Christ saw the multitude of people, he was moved with compassion toward them and blessed them because they were like sheep with no shepherd. Christ is a great entertainer; he was well inclined and cared for the sheep. Lease them, guide them in the right way and, therefore, have a compassion for them. He generously made them his quests and treated them at splendid entertainments so that they might truly be called Christ's disciples. Jesus Christ fed all his guests "Give them to eat." Jesus Christ wants believing Christians to be kind to those who are bad to them; he provided for our daily bread, both good people and bad people. Christ ordered the disciples to give away their food to the poor who had been following him, listening to his word for three days. Jesus Christ came to this universe to be the great feeder. He blessed the bread and two pieces of fish and fed five thousand people and had twelve baskets leftover.

Christ is the great healer and he healed all the people's sickness and diseases. No one was sent away empty or away from Christ, but those that come to him who are already full of themselves.

They have a donation bag where the money people give to them and where they also give out the money to the poor people everywhere the Lord was preaching and teaching (John 12:6, Matthew 26:8-9). Judas Iscariot was the treasurer of Christ during his earthly ministry. He wanted them to sell the oil and give the money to the poor, but not that he really cared for the poor, but because he was a thief and had the bag of money. Judas rather has the money of the oil so that he can put it where he can use it. Christ justified Mary's action as a token of her good will; Christ was well pleased with it. Jesus Christ puts a favorable construction upon what many did, which those who condemned it were not aware or found it hard to see. Providence will open doors of opportunity to good Christians. Those expressions of their life and good deed prove to be more reasonable and more beautiful than anything one can imagine.

Jesus' home in Nazareth was a village occupied by poor agricultural people. When he was born his parents offered the poor people offerings in the temple a poor family sacrifice, which was two doves or two pigeons, but they offered two doves. The offering of a pair of doves indicates that Joseph and Mary were poor according to Old Testament law (Leviticus 12:8). It shows from Jesus' birth onward that he was identified with the poor and underprivileged. Jesus Christ used Peter's mother-in-law's house in Capernaum often as his base after teaching and preaching. Jesus Christ went to Mount Olive after his resurrection because he did not have a home to go to. The King of kings lived on earth like a pauper. Jesus Christ poured out his life for the sinners. When he died, they borrowed a grave in which to lay his body. "It was just before the Passover feast. Jesus knew that the time had come for him to leave this world and go to the Father. Having loved his own who were in the world, he now showed them the full extent of his love" (John 13:1). The Scripture revealed that on the night he was betrayed, Christ washed the feet of his disciples but some of them did not know why Christ was washing their feet. Christ did this for a reason and for good consideration. There are four reasons why Christ washed the feet of his disciples: (1) Christ wanted to show or testify his love for his disciples; (2) Christ wanted to show his humility, which he wanted his disciples to follow after he went back to heaven that he might give an instance of his own voluntary humility; (3) Christ might signify to them spiritual washing, which is referred to in his encounter and discourse with Peter; (4) Christ might set them an example, giving proof of his great love wherewith he loved them and all the people in the world. Christ manifested his love to the disciples by washing their feet. He wanted them to wash each other's feet; as the Lord serving his servants. Christ knows all our infirmities. His loving kindnesses have never failed to this present age.

He was obedient unto death, death of the cross. Apostle Paul made it clear that Christ poured; empty himself in order to purchase us for himself. We Christian believers are now made rich by his poverty, which means we are where Christ was when he was rich and became poor that he might make us rich, which means we too might become poor in order to make those who do not know him rich. Christians reduplicate the life of Jesus Christ's self-giving ministry; we must pour ourselves out to convert souls unto his holy hands. Christians must let others see the life of Christ's glorious miracle of selfgiving, a life of total surrender. Love that transforms and changes life making them rich in Christ from our own riches in Christ show the love of Christ in us to others who do not know him, until we can say Christ in me the hope of glory. Christian believers let us make others rich in him; by our poverty, others might be rich.

When we take our eyes off the whirl of day-to-day activity and concentrate on honoring Him and following in His way, we find a consistent peace that carries us through both plenty and poverty.

—Charles Stanley

CHAPTER THREE
The Sources And Causes Of Poverty

THE BIBLICAL INTERPRETATION OF SOURCES AND CAUSES OF POVERTY

"He who loves pleasure will become poor, whoever loves wine and oil will never be rich." He who works his land will have abundant food, but the one who chases fantasies will have his fill of poverty. To show partiality is not good, yet a man will do wrong for a piece of bread. A stingy man is eager to get rich and is unaware that poverty awaits him. God takes care of those who help the poor and the needy, "The Lord sends poverty and wealth; he humbles and exalts," (Proverbs 21:17, 28:19, 21-22, 1st Samuel 2:7). Some people are very lazy and halfhearted; some people are fools, drunkards, alcoholic, gluttons intentionally eating, a habit that destroys their body and makes them unfit to hold a job. Some people are living a wasteful life that drives them to poverty and makes them very poor. God is saying to us that He allowed us to use the delights of our senses soberly and temperately whereby a wine heart, and oil to make the face shine and beautiful, and everything that causes excessive pleasure shall make him a poor man and he will become a beggar.

Pride also causes people to be poor; they forget about God, who brings them wealth. Hiding sin and sinful nature causes them to become poor. The love of money always brings or results in poverty. If people desire money more than they desire God and kids, they don't care for their family. They will end up poor. The cause of poverty could lead into being selfish and stingy. Inconsiderate behavior causes impoverishment and poverty. Another cause of poverty will be fear. Fear will result in poverty. If people did not want to go anywhere, they are too fearful to go outside and work; it will lead to poverty.

One of the causes of poverty is idleness. Some people prefer to be on welfare instead of working. The welfare system— public assistance— creates idleness and contributes to the corruption of so many behavioral issues. For example, some people were able to work with little experience with many job skills, as well as able to get a small job, but because public assistant encourages idleness in American society, and creates more poverty, even more crimes in some states because of idleness. Most people get into problems in their neighborhood or get into other problems by selling drugs or child trafficking. Idleness turns most people to earn a low income; the system makes the life of some people worse, or worst.

The Scripture revealed that idleness is not of God, "In the name of the Lord Jesus Christ, we command you, brothers, to keep away from every brother who is idle and does not live according to the teaching you received from us." For you yourself know how you ought to follow our example. We were not idle when we were with you (2nd Thessalonians 2:6-7). Apostle Paul said it is the mystery of iniquity already at work in the world through the antichrist, which gradually arrives in the churches of God. The head of the antichrist kingdom is called the "wicked one." Scripture revealed that the Lord would destroy him. The power of the antichrist in due time will soon be totally and finally destroyed, and this will be by the brightness of Jesus Christ's coming. Also, the rule of this man of sin is deceivableness and unrighteousness.

Biblically, those who were idle were people who were lazy and who were unwilling to work; Apostle Paul said idle people need to be disciplined by keeping away from them and not associating with them. The Bible says those who are idle are busybodies in other peoples' lives. They are not working; they walk around the neighborhood chasing women around, and most of the time committing a crime that they wouldn't have committed if they were working. They also engage in domestic violence and neighborhood fights, or stealing, or engage in prostitution of women.

GOVERNMENT PUBLIC BENEFIT CAUSES PROMOTED AND RESULTED IN POVERTY

All these habits are what public assistants are promoting and encouraging. Thank God some states want the welfare recipients to work for their check, which gets many people out of trouble and changes their lives completely. An idle person suffers hunger and has nothing. Laziness is the number one cause of poverty in the lives of human beings. Every house of a lazy person will deteriorate and "slack hands cause poverty." Laziness brings on deep sleep and the shiftless man goes hungry. All work brings a profit, but mere talk leads only to poverty. The sluggard craves and gets nothing, but the desires of the diligent are fully satisfied. "A sluggard does not plow in season; so at harvest time he looks but finds nothing" (Ecclesiastic 10:18, Proverbs 19:15, 14:23, 13:4, 20:4). It was clear biblically that the word of God says laziness results and causes poverty. Lack of work causes slumber in people who are lazy and poverty follows very hard. This says that a sluggish lazy man mindless of his own affairs even of their soul; cast into deep sleep, dreaming, big, but doing nothing, to change their soul from idle and lulled asleep, those that will not labor cannot expect to eat, but must suffer hunger. People who are idle in the affairs of their soul, that take no care or pains to work out their salvation, shall perish because of what is necessary to a life of happiness of the soul.

Those people that will not work, though in the farm cannot expect to reap in times of harvest. They will beg for their food. Aside from ethnic prejudice, oppression, and disobedience as causes of poverty or sources of famine, evidence of impoverishment such as of Ruth and Naomi, or loss of a loved one such as a husband or grown up son, this could be the cause of poverty. The Bible revealed that there was a famine in the land of Israel. Naomi and her husband with their two sons went to Moab. It came to pass that Naomi's husband and her two sons died. Then Naomi said to her sons' two wives to go back to their respective homes, to their parents' homes, "But Ruth replied, don't urge me to leave you, or to turn back from you. Where you go, I will go, and where you stay, I will stay, your people will be my people, and your God will be my God. Where you die I will die, and there I will be buried. May the Lord dealt with me, be it ever so severely, if anything but death separates you and me" (Ruth 1:16-17). Naomi had imparted to Ruth her faith in the Lord God by teaching her about the God of Israel and his love for his people. Ruth's faith in God was developed while living with Naomi and her son through the years, which caused her to remain faithful in her love for Naomi. Ruth illustrated a divine principle that our Lord taught during his earthly ministry, "Whoever loses his life for my sake will find it" (Matthew 10:32). Christ said, whoever as our duty as a Christian, it will be here and after our unspeakable honor and happiness. If we acknowledge Christ before people of this world, it is our greatest duty not only to believe in Christ, but to confess our faith in suffering for him, when there is an opportunity to do so, as well as in his service. Even if we were exposed to shame or reproach and trouble, we shall be abundantly recompensed in heaven. Scripture said, those who honor Christ before men, Christ will honor before his Father; those who disown Christ before men, Christ will disown before his Father on that great day.

"Both Mahlon and Kilion also died, and Naomi was left without her two sons and her husband. To makes ends meet, and find food, "Ruth the Moabitess said to Naomi, Let me go to the fields and pick up the leftover grain behind anyone in whose eye I find favor. Naomi said, 'Go ahead my daughter.' So, she went out and began to glean in the fields behind the harvester. As it turned out, she found herself working in a field belonging to Boaz who was from the clan of Elimelech" (Ruth 1:5, 2:2-3). The spirit of Naomi was active when her husband died and her two sons died. Naomi became poor. Moab gave her a place to live and supplied her whatever she needed. God Almighty God of mercy has mercy on his people. He graciously visited them in time of need and gave them plenty of gifts. God returned Naomi to the land of Bethlehem and sent help to her through her poor daughter-in-law—Ruth. Naomi's condition was very low and she was very poor, which serves as a great trial of faith.

Naomi and her daughter-in-law had no way of getting necessary food they needed to survive; they decided to be gleaning corn on the Boaz farm. Naomi and Ruth believed that God the Father would never fail them and he would never forsake them. Ruth decided to go to the Boaz farm and glean ears of corn. Ruth humbled herself and trusted God. The Scripture revealed that in the Law of Moses God had commanded Israelites to permit the poor and the needy to gather the grain left in the fields after harvest. God wants those who have enough to share with those who have little or nothing. By doing this, Boaz' harvest was blessed and his care for Ruth and Naomi showed that he was a righteous Israelite in the eyes of the Lord.

Ruth's story was one of the stories of God's providence and provision in the lives of all who trust in him and follow his ways. This is in the same way that Abraham responded in faith to God's call. In the same way, Ruth trusted in the Lord who made her leave her country, family and relatives in order to follow his redemptive purpose. Christians should trust and have strong faith in the Lord Jesus Christ.

War is one of the main cause and the number one sources of poverty. When Israelites were in exile, Nehemiah was the cupbearer to the King. A visitor came from Jerusalem and told Nehemiah, "They said to me, those who survived the exile and are back in the province are in great trouble and disgrace. The wall of Jerusalem is broken down, and its gates have been burned with fire" (Nehemiah 1:3). The word was given to Nehemiah by the people who came from Jerusalem. They gave the accounts that the Holy City was desolate and exposed and in ruins. The wall of Jerusalem was broken down. The gates were ruined. The condition of the people was very despicable because of the marks of poverty and slavery. There was no job for people to do. Upon hearing this, Nehemiah was deeply concerned and he wept, mourned, fasted and prayed a prayer that he had never prayed before in his life and God answered the prayers of the poor people and the people who were falling into destruction and hardship in so many areas of their lives.

Israelites were sold into slavery, which was one of the causes of poverty for the people of Israel. "When he heard these things, I sat down and wept.

For some days I mourned and fasted and prayed before the God of heaven" (Nehemiah 1:1-4). God answered Nehemiah's prayers—Nehemiah was commissioned by the King of Persia to go to Jerusalem and rebuild the wall of Jerusalem, which had been broken down after Ezra attempted to rebuild and fortify the city. In spite of much opposition, Nehemiah completed the wall in fifty-two days. Nehemiah was a man of ability, of courage, of perseverance and most especially a man of prayer, who worked hard by prayer to take away the poverty and disgrace from his people of Israel.

SOURCES AND CAUSES OF POVERTY IN THE NATIONS OF THE WORLD

Sources of poverty in all the African nations—the main causes and sources of poverty in each nation of Africa are the basic human needs, which focus all the African nations and societies. There is always a minimum resource for consumption of either food or material things, or physical wellbeing. Extreme poverty and absolute poverty is a condition, which is characterized as a severe deprivation of basic human needs such as food, water, health, shelter, education and good environment such as sanitation facilities.

African nations have many poor among them. Africa is always poor and will continue to be poor because they are not ready to face the reality of helping the poor among them and they are not ready to make changes. Africa will not be rich or the wealth will stay within the political parties. More and more hunger and poverty exist everywhere on the entire continent of Africa. There is also HIV and other diseases that continue to cause death of children. How can they solve the problem of poverty in Africa? Why is it that among all the nations in the world, Africa consists of more poor than any other continent? How can we as individuals, as a corporation, and as organizations help to bring change to all the poor African nations? The political system in African nations must be changed first. They must stop the corruption and greediness and they must care for the poor people among them in their nation. They must be ready to help the poor, instead taking the money, the food and clothing donated for the poor for their personal use, and they must stop selling the clothing that people in another rich country donated for the poor people in their country. According to research, Africa is supposed to be the richest continent in the world, full of oil, copper, gold, diamonds, iron, and all other rich resources but because of greediness and abuse of power, corruption and extremely poor leadership, other countries come and steal all their resources for their own gain.

Selfishness, uncaring attitudes and inconsiderate attitudes for their own people, their own brothers, and sisters their own relatives, father and mother, people are going through a great deal of suffering. The moment the poor vote them into power, they forget what they promised them. All that they care about is how to steal the oil money and take it to another country for their own investment, without thinking that there are many people in the villages and towns who are dying of hunger, lack of medical care, and lack of food for them and for their children. Political people in African nations have no fear of God. Therefore, they don't care what they do to their own people as long as their families are eating good and enjoying life.

Thousands of college students graduated with no job. They are all walking around doing nothing because African nations do not know how to create jobs or they do not want to create jobs. Therefore, unemployment increases where there is no unemployment benefit for those who have no job. African nations are where people are killing their own people because a dictator, a political person, did not want to leave their position. They would rather see many people including children die every day. As long as their own children are saved they care less. The elected presidents of African nations are always for the few people who are close friends and relatives. While children are dying of HIV, other diseases and malnutrition; the scholarships that are supposed to go to poor people for education, political people snatched them and gave them to their own children.

God is the only one who can set up and structure all the African political systems and the political people so that they can know and do the right thing for the poor people in their country. In some other African nations, children are dying of diseases, of the HIV/AIDS epidemic, which affected adults and children continue to increase the population of children in orphanage homes while others die without being seen or treated by any physicians.

World Bank data indicated extreme poverty and analyzed it as the essence of one or more factors enabling individuals and families to assume basic responsibility and to enjoy fundamental rights. The situation may become widespread and could result in more serious and permanent consequences.

The lack of basic security leads to chronic poverty when it simultaneously affects several aspects of people's lives, when it is prolonged and when it severely compromises of regaining their rights and reassuming their responsibilities in the foreseeable future.— Joseph Wresinski 1996

(This was adopted by a UN sub-commission on the promotion and protection of human rights as part of the Despouy Report on Human Rights and Extreme Poverty.)

To eradicate extreme poverty, many organizations from different nations must work to be heard in the areas of poverty. They must set up relief operations, coordinators and humanitarian work to improve the humanitarian efforts and predictability, as well as accountability with the help of international countries to develop better and better humanitarian systems with the individual leaders of that country; representatives and coordinators who can work as a team in order to find firm and constructive ways to eradicate poverty.

We have the United Nations Children's Fund (UNICEF), which was created in 1946 by the United Nations to provide food, clothing, medical or health care services for children who are struggling with famine and diseases. This organization deals primarily with the children in extreme poverty in over ninety countries all over the world helping the children who are going through poverty, violence and diseases. They help children with HIV/AIDS to receive basic education. We also have the UN-Refugee Agency (UNHCR) established December 1950, by the United Nations General Assembly. The organization was established to lead and coordinate international actions that will protect the refugees from problems worldwide.

The primary responsibility is to preserve and safeguard the rights and the wellbeing of refugees in every nation. The organization also must make sure that those refugees who are seeking asylum are safe and help people to restart their lives. They have helped refugees in more than twenty-five countries around the world. We have the World Food Program (WFP). The World Food Program is the world's largest humanitarian services agency fighting hunger worldwide. Their goal is to bring food to more than seventy-five nations who have no food and are in need of food assistance. What happens to this agency is that more than ninety percent of the food in those countries did not reach the poor people of the country.

Those foods are always controlled by the political people of the country and they will not distribute them to the right people. As the WFP responded to emergencies of food supply in order to save lives by supplying them the food, if it is a country where civil war is going on they will not let the food get to the hands of the other side, the opponent they were fighting against. Therefore, many people, including children, will be dying on the other side. This type of incident happened one time in the nation of Sudan. By the time WFP discovered that the food was confiscated by their opponent, many people, especially children, already died.

WFP also works to help the country to prevent hunger in the future through so many programs of storing food. To be more secured they also develop and research with experts and food security analysis for the best solutions for world hunger through poverty.

We also have the World Health Organization (WHO) established to direct and coordinate authority for health within the UN system. Its responsibility is to provide leadership on global health problems—a health research agenda setting standards, maintaining evidence based on policies and options providing technical support to many countries. Monitoring and assessing all the health trends also work to combat diseases such as HIV/AIDS, malaria and tuberculosis, which are causes of poverty, manage safety; work also with newborns and children's health.

We have World Vision, which is a children's humanitarian organization dedicated to work with children, families and their environmental communities worldwide working and tackling the causes of poverty and injustice all over the world. World Vision is working in more than one hundred countries around the world. World vision serves all the people regardless of their religion, race, ethnicity or gender.

Then we have Global Humanitarian Assistance (GHA) The GHA program is to provide an objective in dependent data analysis around the humanitarian financing and the related assistance that developed detail and methodologies for calculating the actual and true value of humanitarian assistance for all the work. GHA is to enable access and shared evidence based on resources in order to meet the needs of the people living in the humanitarian crisis. There should be evidence of reliable information, fundamentally and in accountability to improve the performance. The GHA provide a comprehensive assessment of the international financing response to humanitarian crises. The total cost of each response and where the finance comes from, how much and how they receive it. GHA helps them to find out the financing response measureable to the humanitarian needs. The GHA primary fund comes from donations by society and organizations.

EFFECT OF POVERTY IN AFRICAN CONTINENT

Effects of poverty are primarily poor economic systems all over the African nations—diseases, warfare, civil war, war between nations and political wars that always cause misgovernment and corruption in various ways and in various forms. We can also find poverty in the national accounting system of every nation that will bodily present the nation's expenditure and income activities, measuring and comparing them with other nations' economic abilities. It will also show the quality of life and wellbeing of individuals in the society, for example health care, which means the wealth of the people and job employment of the people in the nation, including the environment, physical and mental health, education, recreation for children, young adults and adults, social change, leisure and quality of life. Africans have very few consumer goods. For example, the Republic of Angola was engaged in civil war from 1975 to 2002. Even though this country has diamond mines, minerals and petroleum reserves, the standard of living remains very low among the population of people in the country. Moreover, infants and children's life expectancy rates are the worst in the nations of the world.

The wealth of the country goes to a small group of people in the country. What is really damaging the continent of Africa is drought and plagues of locusts. Drought, which is the lack of water, either from underground or a surface drought, can go on for months and years in some areas of African nations. This lack of water supply affects the agriculture of the country, which directly affects the economic system of the country. Drought causes the deaths of livestock, animals, birds, chickens and crops. An example is the Sonoran Desert in Mexico. Lack of water causes significant damage such as low productivity of food crops, environmental, agriculture, health, economic and social effects. Some people move to another neighboring country because of no crops, no food and no clean drinking water.

Conflict is another source or cause of poverty. The African continent continually engages in ongoing conflicts of civil war. An example of Somalia and conflicts between the countries of Ethiopia and Eritrea's border, even though these two countries lack basic social services, basic needs of necessities of life, their military forces are always financed and well equipped. The soldiers always have plenty of food to eat while some civilians are dying of hunger. The country of Eritrea is Greek. Its capital is named Asmara. It is bordered by Sudan in the west, Ethiopia coastline along the Red Sea, across from Saudi Arabia and Yemen. Eritrea is a multicultural, multiethnic country recognizing nine ethnic groups. They speak a language called Afro-Asiatic. The civil war between Ethiopia and Eritrea has caused over 100,000 deaths in both countries.

African nations are always full of refugees. They are always displaced by military forces during the times of conflict. Refugees always migrate to open countries such as the United States, Canada, Germany, England, and France. Sometimes, civil war in the country will cause all the government services either to cut down, or be shut down, or closed completely. For example, conflict in the nation of Sierra Leone. This country depends on diamond production, which is the source of the country's economic activity but during the time of conflicts of civil war, it opened the black market, cut down production, which reduces the supply of diamonds, and forced the price to go down because people in another country take advantage of the conflict to create black markets that the government was unable to control. During the civil war, 1,270 primary schools were destroyed. Inflation was over sixty percent between 1990 through 2002. All these were sources and causes of poverty in Sierra Leone.

Sources and causes of poverty were also based on lack of infrastructure; no clean water in most places in African countries, especially in the Sub-Sahara region such as Northern Nigeria and other parts of the Saharan continent, Lagos, Cairo and Kinshasa, Democratic Republic of Congo. Kinshasa, which is the second largest city in Africa after Cairo, is also the second urban area in the world after Paris. Lack of clean water clearly contributed to poverty. Diseases are one of the greatest problems of poverty, diseases that affect infants and children, which are usually caused by lack of clean water, diseases of AIDS in Africa where more than 11,000 are affected and more than 3,000 died. It continues to spread because it is a sexually transmitted disease.

We see causes and sources of poverty through the Ebola virus, malaria through mosquito bites and tuberculosis. Tapeworm is an infection affecting humans and animals caused by raw meat or raw fish consumption resulting from viral infection of bacterial infections and dysentery. Dysentery is an inflammatory disorder of the intestine or colon that results in severe diarrhea, which is very common among young people. They also have sleepy sickness. The Ebola virus causes extreme hemorrhagic fever. This disease is very common in the nation of Zaire. They even named Ebola virus in Zaire, which was derived from the Ebola River, the place of the first outbreak of the disease.

Causes and sources of poverty could happen from human resources such as cheap agricultural and industrial labor and wage practices send people to do the work that machines can do because the industry does not want to buy machines that can do the work. For example, using people to break or pound rocks in pieces with human power and tools instead of machines or using people to be digging in the gold mine or diamond mine instead of using the necessary machine. Nigeria, Sierra Leone and Ghana are examples of African countries that used cheap labor.

Lack of proper education causes and is one of the sources of poverty. Most people in some African nations did not read and have no more than a secondary school education; they work in factories, farms and do maintenance work. Another example of a country with cheap labor is South Africa, especially during apartheid. They barely learned how to speak English and worked primarily in the coalmine.

POVERTY IN THE ASIAN CONTINENT

One of the greatest causes of poverty in South Asian nations is the effects of climate change such as high temperatures, extreme weather problems and rising of the sea level that always results in overflowing of water, intense floods, droughts and storms. Melting of glaciers in the Himalayas increase the floodwater resources, which also compound the natural resources of the area and environment that rapidly affected the urbanization, industrialization and the economic development of South Asian countries. It also decreases crops, causing diarrhea due to floods, storm surge and all other hazards. All these events decrease agricultural productivity, create an impact on the fisheries industry and create an impact on many ecological systems, increasing damage and deaths caused by storm and flood. An increase in incidences of waterborne diseases such as malaria, cholera and more important, decreases in the reliability of the nation's hydropower system and biomass production that also result in the reduction of the economic system of the country.

People from South Asian countries must be preparing for global warming, which is going to be severe. Causes of climate change according to the World Bank sources on climate change are water supply, energy, transport, the mining industry, construction, trade and tariffs, agriculture, forestry and fisheries. Environmental protection and disaster management will assuage great hunger and poverty sources in the world. Managing climate risk integrates adaptation into World Bank group operations. South Asia, which is on the Asian continent—West Asia, Central Asia, East Asia and Southern Asia, the source and causes of poverty in the entire Asian continent are the same. They also have problems with Steppe, which ex tended from one area to another area to the South, which is a semi-desert, and two great rivers, which flow to the Northwest and flow into the sea. Hunger is the world's greatest problem. We also see that in Western Asian countries the causes of poverty are homelessness. People are making a living by collecting and sorting things from the garbage and selling them for money for their daily bread. The same problems exist in North Asia. There is poverty in rural areas among small farmers. The poverty is continuously increasing compared with the overall economic growth. Food and hunger among infants, el elderly, persons with disabilities, insufficient quantity of food and quality that will satisfy the dietary needs of individuals that will be free and acceptable according to their culture—means that those who cannot afford a daily meal, bread, meat, chicken or fish, all these people are at risk and in poverty in Europe. Even though food was being distributed through some organizational aid, it is never enough.

According to the International Convention on Economic and Social Rights, "Every human being has the right to adequate food and the right to be free from hunger"

The price of basic food in Europe has gone sky rocketing. The rate of poverty in counties varies. In the European Union there is more poverty in rural areas and urban communities. Fifty-nine percent of the European Union lives in rural areas and urban communities. There is a big game between the two. Poverty, which is generally associated with agricultural problems as well as unemployment benefits and other social assistance is very low in some countries where agriculture is the main type of employment. Some countries face more agricultural problems than the others do between the farmer and agricultural workers. Fifty percent of adults are poorly educated.

To help the poor among the European Union countries, the price of food must be lower so that the poor people will be able to afford it; also, they must help farmers and the agricultural workers so that unemployment may be reduced. There should be an increase in government aid to the poor, the needy, disabled and senior citizens; they must implore the educational system of each country in East and South Asia. In summary, there is an association between poverty and the rate of employment in Myanmar, but both are very small contributors to overall poverty. Only approximately 2.5% of the poor were unemployed over the past six months. As argued above, poverty has much more to do with low returns to work than with the lack of work.

SOURCES AND CAUSES OF POVERTY IN SOUTH AMERICAN COUNTRIES

According to Poverty in America: Causes and Sources of Poverty in America, the United States poverty level, characterized and categorized have the amount of education even though the majority of people in America were educated through government grants and loans. Those who are poor in America are mostly uneducated, with no job skills; no job experience and they lack intelligence. The second main source of poverty in America is people with disability, people with health problems and various kinds of health issues and handicapped people who live beyond their income benefits that the government provides (SSI benefits). The third source and cause of poverty is the senior pension and Social Security Retirement benefits, which is never enough for some senior citizens because it was based on their salary before they retired.

Some people are poor because they believe that certain people discriminate against them by color, race, or gender. Therefore, they refuse to work. Second, agricultural problems up and down that always affect produce of fruits, vegetables and livestock. When this happens, many families will lack foods, meat, chicken and other resources, which are needed to meet their minimum daily nutritional needs.

America has its own climate change problems; whereby, climate changes contributed to an increase in food prices as well as a shortage of food. Climate changes affected food items such as rice, grains, fruits and wheat, which are the most important foods for a majority of the people in America and in South American countries.

Other sources and causes of poverty in America are droughts and floods, including wildfire that causes immediate destruction. For example, hurricanes that destroys all animals and crops when struck by natural disasters, which were called acts of God by insurance companies. In addition, earthquakes and volcanos can causes planes to stop flying from one destination to another and affect company business. Not only American business suffers from national disasters but other countries in the world go through the same thing in a different time of day and year. Houses and businesses were damaged and people were rendered homeless.

SOURCES AND CAUSES OF POVERTY IN SOUTH AMERICAN COUNTRIES

Poverty in South American counties is very high compared to other countries. Poverty affects all the South American countries at a higher rate even though these countries all have experience of growth in their economies and they all are trying to reduce the level of poverty in their society but there is still plenty more work to do. To stabilize the life of people, for example, people in Argentina and all other neighboring countries were facing housing problems. Living conditions of people are very bad. Lack of medical insurance is another cause and source of poverty in all South American countries. Bolivia is one of the poorest countries in South America. It shows that more than sixty percent of the people in Bolivia were going through extreme poverty, which was caused by lack of electricity and lack of clean water.

Brazil also has a high poverty rate. Millions of Brazilians live on two dollars per day and millions make less than one dollar per day. Moreover, Brazil has the most unique income distribution in the world. The country of Colombia has some of the most extreme poverty in South America. They also have a high crime rate in the country. Both in rural areas and in the urban areas, people are going through various forms of suffering. The country has been trying their best to reduce poverty by creating more development that is educational and creates jobs. With a small population, the country of Ecuador only has a high level of poverty in rural areas. The sanitation system and clean water system in the poverty area is poor. The country suffers from low job income, a poor educational system, as well as poor teaching skills, especially in rural areas. Countries continue to increase in population to the point that some cities are very overpopulated and overcrowded. Millions of Peruvians are still suffering from poverty. Other nations are struggling to solve the poverty rate, but the people need free health care. They have a high rate of unemployment but the poverty rate is going lower than in other South American countries.

Even though the country of Venezuela is rich in natural resources, the people continue to suffer from a high level of poverty, which is more than thirty percent. Venezuela provided free health care for its people, which help to relief the poverty rate in the country. In South America, people are very unhappy because of the causes of poverty. There is a high level of fertility drug addiction, which is another cause of poverty, as well as environmental problems. Food supply is barely enough for the people of all South American countries, more so in urban slums.

Natural disasters such as hurricanes, which always claim the lives of many people, cause more poverty in South American counties in the area of Honduras and Nicaragua. In Panama, poverty affected more than ninety percent of the people. El Salvador poverty is forty-eight percent in the rural areas. Costa Rica maintains a lower level of poverty, which is approximately thirty-five percent. In Mexico, forty-five percent suffer poverty because of lack of food and other crops; especially the reduction of prices of crops such as maize and rice makes half of the farmers extremely poor. The two biggest countries in North America are the United States and Canada. The poverty rate is thirty-seven percent in rural areas with poverty rates in children higher than urban community families. The rate is higher in racial and ethnics groups, more between Hispanics, Blacks and American Indians.

We think sometimes that poverty is only being hungry, naked and homeerty.

—Mother Theresa

CHAPTER FOUR
Is Poverty The Act Of God?

Poverty is never and will never be an act of God because God is love; he loved us to the point that he sent his only begotten Son to deliver us from sin and death and all the nature of sin. Most of the poverty in the world was caused by what we do to ourselves. In the community, between individuals from one community to another community, within each state, between states, to the nations. What we did caused damage, wars and all others, things that cause poverty from one household to another household.

Poverty is not an act of God; according to UN hunger relief statistics, over 980 million people in this world are chronically malnourished or undernourished. Thousands of children are dying every day due to poverty, lack of food and lack of medical care, hunger and diseases. Many Christian organizations responded to help those who are in pain, suffering and dying of hunger because of medical care but they do not have enough food to eat. A nation's governing body must be able to help the poor among them by using the money from the country's resources to create more jobs and more medical services but instead of that they always ship the money to another country rather than invest it in their own account and name while innocent children, young adults, adults, and senior citizens are dying with hunger in their own nation. The people who are corrupt and put the money in their name when they die, the money perishes in the bank of the nation where they invest the money because no one knows the bank account number except them.

The Scripture revealed, "For I know the plans I have for you, declares the Lord, plans to prosper you and not to harm you, plans to give you hope and a future. Then you will call upon me and come and pray to me, and I will listen to you. You will seek me and find me when you seek me with all your heart" (Jeremiah 29:11-13). God is telling prophet Jeremiah that he knows the thoughts that he had for him—which is the same for us today. God's thoughts are good toward his children to the very end of their life, which he will give according to his plan at his time. People of this earth, especially the children of God, must be patient until the appointed time when the fruit is ripe and then they shall eat it. When their life is at its worst, he will give them glorious perfection of their deliverance. God almighty that is the beginning and also the end, finished and completed what he started in the lives of his children. All the heavenly hosts and the people of the earth will bring to completion all the blessings of his people; he will give them the expectations of their faith in him. God said, "You shall find me when you seek me with all your heart" (Verse 13).

Prophet Jeremiah prophesied to the people of Israel that at the end of the seventy years of captivity, a new fullness of time would occur; God would move within a holy remnant of Israelites so that they would seek him in prayer with all their hearts. God will listen, and answer from heaven and fulfill his promises of restoration.

The same things are going on in our world today, until one of the dictators or presidents of the nations comes to his or her senses that he is going to leave this earth one day, and begin to show love to those who elected him in his position, planning good things for the children, the people and everyone in that nation, poverty will continue to destroy the life of every human being in their own country and in the hands of their own people. For example, with all the oil money in the country of Nigeria West Africa, Nigeria has over 579 billion dollars in the Federal Reserve Bank; still, his people are begging for food. There are no proper medical services in the towns and villages, no electricity, no clean water in all the rural and urban areas. Millions of students graduated. There is no job. They refused to create jobs for their college graduates. States' governing authorities are transporting beggars, the disabled, orphans, homeless, and those who are suffering from mental illness from state to state instead of caring for them. The state governments have enough money that the federal government has allocated for them to take care of the poor, the needy, the homeless, the disabled and the children who are in need of proper medical care, food and clothing. The state governments are not using the money for the poor and what they are doing with the money is a big question.

I pray that the state government in Nigeria will stop their inhuman behavior, cruel activities of evil and begin to care for the poor among them, instead of violating their human rights. Those who wanted to care for the beggars are not even allowed to help them, because they are continuously moving, dumping, transporting the poor, homeless people from one state to another state as if they are garbage. These people might be poor but they are the citizens of Nigeria. The state governors must remember that the poor among them are all children of God, and they too might become poor and homeless tomorrow and they might be in need of help. If not food, it could be medical help.

Poverty is not an act of God. The political government makes it look like it is the act of God. After the Nigerian people vote the political people into power, they quickly come up with abusive of power by implementing so many things that are not helping the poor, the needy and the people who vote them to power. The poor people in the country will continue to suffer; they are dying because people in the government do nothing to help them.

Government policies also created more economic problems that resulted in poverty on so many levels of the nation's economy and government misuse of national resources such as oil, uranium, gold, diamond, copper, iron, and etcetera. Government people and corruption from people in high places and high positions because more poverty to the people who have no means of making ends meet. There is a lack of educational services, lack of medical services and lack of medicine for people who are sick. Some people wanted to work in order to make a daily living but they were unable to get a job. The employed people also look for so many ways in order to get a better job to no avail. Some of them try to sell some things by the side of the street. There are many online businesses but it is not a true business. Some people pay to get an online job. They find out that after paying for the registration that the business is not a legitimate business or it does not generate any income.

Most of the online businesses are not genuine and they are not registered with the state, or they have no license. Therefore, if you lost money to register with them you cannot take them to court, and if you take them to court, you might not win. Suffering diseases, poverty and inequality between the rich and the poor are not caused by God and they are not the acts of God. Humanity has replaced God with all the wealth and material things of this world. Therefore, God leaves them alone.

God's wrath is against all the inhabitants of this world. Scripture revealed, "The wrath of God is being revealed from heaven against all the godlessness and wickedness of men who suppress the truth by their wickedness, since what may be known about God is plain to them, because God has made it plain to them. For since the creation of the world God's invisible qualities his eternal power and divine nature have been clearly seen, being understood from what has been made, so that men are without excuse" (Roman 1:18-20). Scripture revealed that the light of nature and the light of the law of God revealed God's anger against the sins of people. The sinfulness of men consists of ungodliness and unrighteousness. The causes of human sinfulness are holding the truth as a prison so that it should not influence them. The unrighteous wicked evil heart is like a dungeon, which like many good things, the truth about God was buried; not in the word of God only, but in God's providences, his judgments upon the sinners are revealed from heaven. This is the reason why Scripture, said the knowledge of God, was known by men. This implies that things of God may be apprehended, but human beings cannot comprehend it; the finite understanding of God cannot be perfectly known. God Almighty imputed in the heart of men his own nature, by what he created, the invisible things of God, even his eternal power and Godhead. The powers of the Godhead are invisible things clearly seen in their created state; and this is the power of the Godhead and the knowledge that was sufficient to keep people out of idolatry.

The worker is known by his own work. God's plan in our lives; every day abundant proof of God as the creator, his beauty of the universe, abundantly proves for his eternal, power and Godhead. People of this earth must know that the way to know God is by the truth of God revealed in the scriptures. The Bible is telling us in this world that the wrath or anger of God is an expression of his righteousness and his holiness. God is grief and anger because human to human wickedness, wicked behavior from individuals to nations is unjust. Unrighteous of human beings unloved, selfishness, uncared for the welfare of other human beings, hatred toward each other, plan of evil toward each other, these are all sin and it causes death and poverty in the world.

God gave up the wicked people over to uncleanness and impassion. Ruin and death comes to those who disobey God, those who said there is no God. Honor God, obey God. We will be able to express that love to all other people in other nations in need of help. The Bible continues to say that there is going to be a day of judgment for the ungodly and the wicked people of this world. God is very concerned about what we are doing to ourselves; he sent his only begotten Son Jesus Christ to us, to save us, redeem us from our sins and bless us with a new life in him. However, we rejected him. We did not listen to him. The Scripture revealed, "He was in the world, and though the world was made through him, the world did not recognize him. He came to that which was his own, but his own did not receive him. Yet to all who received him, to those who believed in his name, he gave the right to become children of God" (John 1:10-12). Jesus Christ came to this world in our own form; he took our nature upon him and dwelt among us. Christ was in the world but not of it. The greatest thing of honor that was ever put on this world was the Son of God came to the world. The world was made by him. Therefore, he came to the world to save, which was lost because it was a world made by him. The world he made did not know him.

When Christ shall come as a judge the world will know him then. He came to his own; his own did not welcome him or receive him. However, as many received the Son of God, he gave them permission to become a child of God. The true Christians' description and poverty is that they receive Christ and believe in his name. Believing in Jesus Christ's name is receiving him as a gift from God. Christians must receive Christ's doctrine as a true word of God and good. They must receive the image of his grace, and impressions of his love, as the governing principle of our affections for Christ's actions.

The world did not want to know God, acknowledge God or recognize God. This means that the entire society of people in this world are doing their own thing, operating independently of God, in his word and in his rules over the universe that he created. The world also has never recognized Jesus Christ; they remain indifferent, or they are the energy of God in Christ and his gospel, and they will remain so until the end of this world when Christ returns. Therefore, whatever is happening in the world, we cause to ourselves by not loving each other.

Poverty is not the act of God; it could be eradicated completely if we love ourselves beginning from individuals to nations. As I am writing this book, UN refugee relief is working hard to feed millions of people including children who flee from their home because of war in Syria. Their own army is fighting and killing their people, which they are supposed to protect. They are killing them with chemical weapons, which kill millions of children and adults.

The Scripture says there is going to be a new heaven and a new earth where righteousness will reign, "But in keeping with his promise we are looking forward to a new heaven and a new earth, the home of righteousness" (2nd Peter 3:13). Christian believers must be looking into the new heaven and a new earth where righteousness dwells—those things that we see how just very soon pass away and are no more and they will not continue on a new earth. All the Christians are urged to be looking for and hoped for earnestly. Expect the new earth, believers must rejoice in hope of more glorious heavens after these have been refined by that dreadful fire, which shall burn up all this visible creation, which the true Christians are looking for. In the new heavens and the new earth, only righteous people shall dwell there forever.

Where there will be no presidents, no dictator and no human control, God will live among his people forever—Jesus is the prince of peace and our hope of glory. Come quickly Lord Jesus.

Almost half of the population of the world lives in rural regions and mostly in a state of poverty. Such inequalities in human development have been one of the primary reasons for unrest and, in some parts of the world, even violence.

—Abdul Kalam

CHAPTER FIVE
The Role Of The Rich To The Poor

Right from the Scripture, God wants those who have to care for those who do not have because of so many circumstances that brought poverty to individual lives and to the country. God appointed the United Nations to see that every inhabitant of the earth is well cared for beginning from their family to the people in their neighborhood who are struggling and do not have any means of food and are dying of hunger or so many various diseases.

Poverty is growing through the various disasters such as hurricane, flood, volcano, earthquake, wildfire, storm and heat waves. The role of the rich is voluntarily to offer to help the people. Most of the time it will be better for the rich to visit the place and see what they can do by themselves instead of giving money to some relief organizations that will not give the money to the poor people or spend seventeen cents of a dollar for the victim. Some of all these life organizations did not even give the poor any money. It is like a business where they pocket money.

Another role of the rich could be to create jobs whereby people will have a job and the poverty level of the state or country will be changed and immediately poverty will be reduced. The role of the rich among the poor in any nation is to look for the poor and see what they can do for them. I have seen some rich people. They have what they call The Food on the Wheel where they go from neighborhood to neighborhood during lunch hour and distribute hot meals to the poor, children and adults in the neighborhood who have no food or proper nutritional food to eat.

This type of program will help the poor in every nation, if the rich people can engage in it or if they can also distribute clothes and sneakers to the children before every school year begins. This will motivate the poor children to study very hard in school. I strictly advise the rich to seek and make every effort to find out what type of role they want to engage in to help the poor among us.

The rich should look for an opportunity to have a role in the poverty reduction of the nation, especially in underdeveloped countries. Also in a country where there is always civil war between nations and natural disasters such as hurricanes, storms, volcanos erupting and lack of medical help for the children to correct disabilities that they cannot afford to do in their own country.

The role of the rich to the poor is continually to offer to help in any area of this world. The rich can also engage in the energy programs where there is no electric power, no water and no medical supply. They must be ready to help educate those who have no money for college and offer them scholarships to those kids so that they can be able to have good education and then reduce poverty.

Focusing your life solely on making a buck shows a certain poverty of ambition. It asks too little of yourself. Because it's only when you hitch your wagon to something larger than yourself that you realize your true potential.

—Barack Obama

CHAPTER SIX
How Can The Rich Help The Poor

All the rich CEOs of the banks and corporations can decide to split their salary in half and give to the poor. They also can create jobs and hire more people.

There are so many ways that the rich could help the poor. There are many reasons why the rich people in a poor country should help the country instead of building up nuclear weapons against each other, weapons of mass destruction and fighting unnecessary wars.

They can use the money to help the poor countries that are in need of water, electric energy supplies, food and all other medical items that can stabilize the lives of many children as well as unborn children, adults, seniors and people of various kinds of disabilities in the world. Instead of using the soldiers to fight war, they should use them to fight the war of hunger and the war of clean energy and clean water supply. Whereby they will actually, physically go there and help them with farming, all other things in school, all other training aspects in technology and in so many other things that can help the people of that poor nation.

There are so many other things such as helping them to plant crops, farm works, drilling for water, that can help the people of a poor nation, instead of in war zones fighting a war; the entire poor country will turn around from poverty and the poverty will be completely reduced or eradicated. Moreover, there will be more love from country to country that everyone will be so comfortable in their own country and there will be no problem of people risking their lives to cross from Mexico to America. The country that offered to send their Army to fight the war of hunger will be richer in resources and the trade between the countries will be strong and solid. The rich must have to make it a matter of responsibility

bility to help developing and underdeveloped countries; its people are suffering and dying every day from famine, diseases, drought, war and all other disasters.

Money donated to the government of a poor country does not get to the people of that country; it goes to the government and the political people. They use it for nuclear weapons and weapons of mass destruction while the poverty continues and the poor are dying for lack of food and all other human needs. The rich country could send their own soldiers and show the poor country how to get water, install hydroelectric devises, water supplies, help them do farming and agricultural work, help in animals and increase production of other livestock. The lives of the people will be better and they will turn around and be useful to developing and rich countries. If they build industrial projects that will create more jobs for the people of that country, it will be great to help them rather than fighting wars. People are fighting, losing their life for unnecessary fights or a piece of land.

The rich country helping the poor or poverty stricken country will create more love, more peace between countries and it will help to link all the countries of the world together in one bond of piece as God created the world to be from the beginning of the creation of the world. This will also help every country to trade their goods and material wealth with each other, just as cell phones and the Internet are connecting the people of the world together (technological innovation). Countries should help each other to fight poverty. Goods from poor countries will be able to have a chance and people will learn how to eat different foods from one country to another country. No one will get tired of eating food from their own country alone. For example, when I traveled to the United Arab Emirates, I saw MacDonald's and other American food there; it was a big relief that even though I am not home, I can still eat my favorite food in a foreign country.

The rich country must also adopt the law of God that says if anyone poor owed you money for seven years and that person cannot pay it, cancel the debt; erase whatever he owed you and forgive him. If you can still help him or her, do so. Nations must write off any amount that the poor nation owed them; especially the World Bank, they must write off the money owed by the poor countries. Rich countries must explore how to reduce the suffering in the lives of the people in the poor nations. They must concentrate on human needs to preserve lives of people instead of fighting wars. The United Nations cannot, and are unable to, fight the war of hunger in all the nations of earth alone; it is impossible for them to do so. Every nation must get involved. That is the only way it could be done.

Give billions of dollars to the country for the poor. The government does not help the people in the country. The political people in the government will pocket the money for their own use; the poor will continue to suffer. It goes to the mouth of the corrupt people in the government of the country. Sometimes, some equipment will be lying down without use or they don't have people who are trained to use it.

We all wish to live. We all seek a world in which men are freed of the burdens of ignorance, poverty, hunger and disease. And we shall all be hard-pressed to escape the deadly rain of nuclear fall-out should catastrophe overtake us.

—Haile Selassie

CHAPTER SEVEN
God's Role To The Poor

The Scripture revealed God's role to the poor. It is very clear, and simple that we must help the poor. God wants us to show love and care for our neighbor, including loving the foreigners and resident aliens who come to live in our community. Jesus Christ gave us the parable of the Good Samaritan, "On one occasion an expert in the law stood up to test Jesus. Teacher, he asked, what must I do to inherit eternal life? What is written in the Law? He replied. How do you read it? He answered; Love the Lord your God with all your heart, with all your soul, with all your strength, and with your entire mind and love your neighbor as yourself. You have answered correctly, Jesus replied. Do this and you will live. However, he wanted to justify himself, so he asked Jesus, and who is my neighbor? In reply, Jesus said, a man was going down from Jerusalem to Jericho, when he fell into the hands of robbers. Go and do likewise" (Luke 10:25-37). A man of law was asking Christ what good he could do in his life in order to attain eternal life. The lawyer stood up and asked Jesus what I shall do to inherit eternal life. Christ knows the intent of the lawyer's heart. He answered him according to the wisdom and goodness; he answered him with a question "What is written in the law? How readest thou?" (Verse 26). Christ made him know himself; how he studied his profession would inform him and he allowed him to practice according to his knowledge, so that he could find his answer to eternal life. This will be of great use for us today, on our way to heaven, if we consider what is written in the Old Testament law, and we read it.

The parable of the Good Samaritan emphasizes inherent in true saving faith and obedience is compassion for those in need. The call to love God is a call to love other people, especially people who are jobless, homeless, distressed or suffering from diseases. The new life and grace that Christ gives to those who accept him will produce love, mercy and compassion for those who are in need and those who are afflicted, rejected and suffering.

God says it is the responsibility of all born again Christian believers to act on the Holy Spirit's love within them and not to harden their hearts to those who are in need. The true believers must not harden their hearts under any circumstances or be insensitive to the suffering and needs of others. Our neighbors are those who need our help in order to survive all that they were going through at that particular time; it is in our power to help them.

God's commandment is that we just don't help only our neighbor but anyone we have contact with, we come to know, not just someone who lives near us. We must always show our love, our concern and our compassion for the welfare of that person. "If you show special attention to the man wearing fine clothes and say, here's a good seat for you, but say to the poor man, you stand there or sit on the floor by my feet, have you not discriminated among yourselves and become judges with evil thoughts?" (James 2:3-4). Christian believers must not show respect to Christians for anything so much as their conformity to Christ. We should not show respect to a person in a way that lessens the glory of our Lord. Christians must not behave to one another according to their appearance. God has his remnant people among the poor and the needy. In the eyes of the Lord, rich and poor are the same and on the same level. No rich man is set close to the lord because of his riches

God is displeased with those people who always show favoritism, who give special attention to people because of their riches and wealth or because of their social standing, or position such as people in high government positions. God says this attitude is wrong for so many reasons because people are looking at the outward appearance but they are not looking at the heart.

It is not motivated by true and genuine love for poor people in society. "Everyone must submit himself to the governing authorities, for there is no authority except that which God has established. The authorities that exist have been established by God. Consequently, he who rebels against the authority is rebelling against what God has instituted, and those who do so will bring judgment on themselves" (Romans 13:1-2). God wants all Christian believers to submit themselves, to conduct themselves toward the governing authority, their authority and their dignity. Christians must submit to the government law and order, and they must obey the government.

At the same time, the Lord said let every human soul be subjected to one another including the ministers of the word, the preachers; subjection must be voluntarily, sincerely, free and must be from the heart. The subjection of the souls of Christians required inward honor and outward reverence and respect in everything they do or say. Christ gave them an example. He was reproached and smitten. He did not say a word.

There is no power but of God. God is the sole ruler of this world. He ordained the government to control the unruly and the evil people to set up rules and regulations and peace. God's wisdom, power, mercy and goodness lie in the management of mankind, human beings, whatever the government is doing, it is always in an ordinance of God and it is to be received by the people and must be submitted that who so ever resists the power of government, resists the ordinance of God. Judges and magistrates, in a more peculiar manner, are God's servants. God commanded all the Christian believers to obey the state government, for the state as an institution is ordained and established by God.

God has instituted the government because in this world we need certain restraints and rules that will protect the people from the various chaos and lawlessness that naturally come with some forms of sin. Therefore, the civil government is also under the law of God to preserve the right, the dignity and the life of the poor people, sick people and distressed people. They must make sure that they are receiving or treating them well, as they should other people in the society.

This made God's role concerning the poor more clearly. The government must be responsible for the poor of their nation and make it an utmost priority to feed those who are hungry, supply food, water supply, energy supply and medical supply. If any government fails to meet this obligation for the people of their country, they abandon them and if they fail to make it part of their operation and function, they are no longer operating according to God's purpose and standard. Those who are in the government body might face the judgment of God. "What good is it, my brothers, if a man claims to have faith but has no deeds? Can such faith save him? Suppose a brother or sister is without clothes and daily food. If one of you says to him, Go, I wish you well; keep warm and well fed, but does nothing about his physical needs, what good is it? In the same way, faith by itself, if it is not accompanied by action is dead" (James 2:14-16). God wants all the people in this world to speak and act in order to correct what needs to be corrected in our society. God is especially telling all the Christians in the church and everywhere to help those who are in need of help in every nation. By doing this, our faith in God will be more strengthened and God will really know that we love him.

If we profess to have saving faith in the Lord Jesus Christ but we have nothing to show for it, no evidence of our sincere devotion to him, to his word and to the people that he wants us to care for, we are not practicing what we are preaching or what has been preached to us. The word of God is manifest in the hearts. Christians in the world must show more compassion for the poor and the needy. They must make all effort to feed the hungry soul with spiritual food, which is the word of God and with physical food, which will make them stay alive. It is part of Christian obedience to Jesus Christ when they care for the needy, the sick and disabled people in the society. "If anyone considers himself religious and yet does not keep a tight rein on his tongue, he deceives himself and his religion is worthless. Religion that God our Father accepts as pure and faultless is this; to look after orphans and widows in their distress and to keep oneself from being polluted by the world" (James 1:26-27). The blessedness of God does not lie in knowing, but in doing the will of the Father. It is not talking, but walking, that will bring the believers to heaven.

Christians must be able to distinguish between fake and vain religion from pure and approved religion, which is from God. When people think that they are more religious than others, it is a sign that their religions are but vain, because in a vain religion people judge and look down on each other; they find faults in others and they believe they are wiser than and better than other Christians. This is purely a vain fake religion. People with a detracting tongue cannot exercise a truly humble gracious heart. In a vain religion, men deceive their own hearts. The true religion consists of the pure and undefiled, a holy life full of glory and a loveable pure heart that shows a true religion. This religion is pure, and undefiled, which is before God the Father; it is a religion that teaches Christians to do well, as in the presence of the Lord. It is a religion that exercises compassion and love to the poor, the needy and the distressed from a very great part of true religion. It is a religion that visits the fatherless and the widow in their troubles and afflictions. By this religion, we will be able to understand all who are proper objects of love, all who are in affliction.

Apostle James is telling us that the genuine and true religion of those who claim to be religious must be defined in a way that a professed Christian must be willing and voluntarily show love to the orphans, children with no father and mother, a widow who have no one to care for her, who are in need of food supplies as well as medical supplies, people who have no one to care for them at all in this world.

Believers were expected to show them the same care and love that God shows toward the fatherless and the widow. Christians should seek the needy and alleviate their distress, thereby showing them that God cares for them. God's role was very clear, my brothers and sisters, in the book of proverbs "If a man shuts his ears to the cry of the poor, he too will cry out and not be answered" (Proverbs 21:13). Uncharitable people of this world who turn their ears off to the cry of the poor and the needy, send them away empty handed from their door and shut the bowels of their compassion. They shall be reduced to nothing, which will turn them around as well as make them cry. God will reward them as they reward the poor in times of their trouble. God will not have mercy upon them for they show no mercy for the poor.

If we want God to bless us, to hear our prayers when we are in need in any area of our lives, we must be willing and able to hear the cry of the poor people who are suffering in various areas of their lives and respond with love to their needs and try our best to help them. God will turn around and bless us, help us in all areas of our lives.

We need to steer clear of this poverty of ambition, where people want to drive fancy cars and wear nice clothes and live in nice apartments but don't realize their full potential.

—Barack Obama

CHAPTER EIGHT
The Poors Must Do Their Own Part

The number of people who are suffering in the world because of hunger, water illnesses and diseases are growing every day. The number is over one billion.

Global food prices are beginning to fall and sometimes climb up again. Small farmers are ready to work harder if there is financial help in South Africa, Sahara, and South Asia and around the world. Farmers are ready to increase the productivity of their crops, if every government is ready to train the farmers on how to use the farming equipment for modern agricultural production, as the poor people in a country with poverty will learn how to use the equipment instead of sowing seeds with their own hands. There will be a greater increase in food production in those countries for the poor people to eat. Millions will move out of poverty. What happens is that some of the people donated manufacture agricultural equipment to developing and under developing countries but it was just piled up in the warehouses. They did not give it out to the farmers to use. It is their farms just because they do not want to set up training or send people to train these people in rural areas and villages how to use the equipment. Until each governmental body is ready to train people in their country on how to use agricultural equipment on the farm there is still going to be a shortage of food. There are people who are willing to help the farmers grow crop, take care of livestock such as cows, chickens and all the food items of that nation; it will be very difficult to solve poverty problems if people are not willing to work hard.

If there is help from the government sector— money given to political people cannot solve the problems. They might use the money for their own gain and the hungry will continue to go hungry. Farmers will be able to use modern equipment for growing their maize and wheat. Doctors will come from all other parts of the world to help or train other people to be veterinarians so that they can know how to apply vaccine and other medicines that protect the livestock in the poor nations.

The country will have plenty of food and they will be able to sell the surplus to another country. Before you know it, lives of the people in the poor countries will turn around for the better and all the people will be happy when they have plenty of food to eat and clean water to drink. According to my interviews with the farmers in other countries, they are ready to welcome those who wanted to help them. Veterinary vaccines and other medicines will clear diseases that could have an affect on cattle, sheep, goats, as well as chickens; there will be plenty of eggs to eat and there will be meat for every household to cook for their meals. Poverty will be reduced; the poor will be able to make a living as well as make changes in their lives.

If they vote for a better political party during the political election of their country, a new political party might be ready to help the poor more than the former political party. Votes of the poor people are very important during the governmental elections. The poor must make all efforts to change; this will bring great changes to any poor country and bring stability to each individual person in the country. The poor must make it their responsibility to vote during the election of their country in order to have a change in life. Poor people's votes are very valuable just as the rich people's votes are valuable. A hospital must be willing to spread to villages and towns instead of located only in the big city alone. They must be willing to spread to all the rural, urban and local areas where people are in need of medical care and they must train people of that village to know how to use all the medical equipment that can help the people during any emergencies. Transporting the poor to the city causes more death in rural areas just because they did not have proper equipment to treat the person.

The poor are ready to change if all these changes mentioned could be implemented by the federal, state and city government of each country. The other important thing is that the poor must examine themselves and find out those things they are doing such as bad habits that are not good for them and cause them to lose their job or makes them sick; they must also reevaluate, as well as prioritize and make a good decision to bread away or stay away from habits that cause them problems, those things that do not help them to live healthy lives. Pay more attention to anything that can make them unable to work. An unhealthy lifestyle that devastating and results in destruction for the body. They must be ready to stop doing the same thing over and over again even though they knew that it is not good for their body, soul and spirit. They must be willing to change from bad habits good habits.

Poor people must make sure to live happy lives that everyone expected. They should change their living environment as well as make new friends. Poverty has become more and more widespread in many countries, especially in African counties in this century. Because extreme poverty is increasing in most parts of the world, this is making it as if it is impossible to challenge the development of poverty in each country or from one country to another country.

Some poor people are ready and willing to change but in a country with climate changes, it is impossible without government intervention. Climate changes crippled the poor to make changes in their lives, especially where there is wildfire. All the firms were burned out. Their entire houses were burned out, including the crops, animals and livestock. It is very difficult for the individual poor who wanted to make a change to find a job in a firm where there is no more work because the firm has been burned out by wildfire.

The world is very different now. For man holds in his mortal hands the power to abolish all forms of human poverty, and all forms of human life.

—John F. Kennedy

CHAPTER NINE
The Rich Must Learn How To Redistribute Wealth

The Scripture said, "Command those who are rich in this present world not to be arrogant nor to put their hope in wealth, which is so uncertain, but to put their hope in God, who richly provides us with everything for our enjoyment. Command them to do good, to be rich in good deeds, and to be generous and willing to share" (1st Timothy, 6:17-18). The rich people of this world must not be proud or arrogant or put their hope in their riches, which are unstable and uncertain. They must put their lives and their hopes in God, who is the provider of the riches and all wealth.

Apostle Paul wrote the young Timothy to warn those who are rich in this world to be careful about the temptation and improve the opportunities of their prosperous riches. Rich people must be humble and not exercise pride. Also, he warned them not to put their confidence in their riches but in God who gave to everyone liberally. He also told Timothy to remind those who are rich they must know that God is the one who make them rich and makes a provision for them to enjoy their wealth. They must do good with their wealth. They must do good with their riches, and they must try to be rich in good works of love and must always prepare to help the needy and the poor. Servants of the Lord must not be afraid of the rich people. They must warn them against pride and more greediness for money.

He provides everything for a reason, so that we may be able to know him better. Rich people must learn how to do good not taking advantage of the poor. God wants the rich to be rich in doing good things for their business partners, for the people they don't even know. God wants them to give to the poor generously and to give to the needy according to their need. God wants them to give cheerfully not sparingly. He wants them to help those who are in need of medical care, the sick and disabled among them. God does not want the rich people of this world to be high minded or to trust in their uncertain riches or wealth. He wants them to put all their trust on the one and only the ever-living God.

Nothing is more uncertain than the riches of the world; people could have plenty today and all could be gone tomorrow. Rich people must know that their riches come from God, not through their own power. It was given to them by God who created all things for us to enjoy in this world because many people have riches but they do not enjoy it. They live in fear that its light might be gone at anytime. They are scared to even spend more or give money to anyone. They have no sincere heart to brighten their wealth. However, they must do good and share their wealth. However, if they do good and share their wealth with the poor and the needy freely and willingly they will be happy persons, living with joy every day. They will be happy to pay the right wages to those who are working for them.

"Do not store up for yourselves treasures on earth, where moth and rust destroy and where thieves break in and steal. However, store up for yourselves treasures in heaven, where moth and rust do not destroy and where thieves do not break in and steal. For where your treasure is, there your heart will be also" (Matthew, 6:19-21). Jesus Christ warned all those who believed in him not to covet the praise flattering of men, or the wealth of this world and we Christians must not chose the world as people in the world because it will lead to fundamental error and makes them guilty of the world for their reward. Christ warned not to lay treasure on earth where all could be destroyed or liable to loss or decay, but to lay treasure in heaven where it will be preserved securely. Christ warned that worldly wealth has in itself principles of corruption and decay from all forms of violence. Christ wants all to give diligence to make sure that it is our wisdom to lay our treasures to eternal life through Jesus Christ and to depend upon our happiness, and look upon all things with a holy contempt. Believers must trust God to keep our treasures safe for us. It is a great encouragement to lay up our treasure in heaven where it is happiness above and beyond measure, the changes and channels of time, the inheritance that is incorruptible.

Our Lord and Savior Jesus Christ spoke clearly and affirmed many times on many occasion about riches and poverty. He said, "Blessed are the poor in spirit, for theirs is the kingdom of heaven" (Matthew, 5:3). Jesus Christ's Sermon on the Mount was full of blessings because Christ came to this world to bless us with his abundant blessings. We have to notice that the Old Testament ended with a curse but the Gospel of God in the New Testament started with blessings. Every blessing pronounced has a double intention, to show an account and what true happiness consists of. Blessedness is what Christians and people of this world pretend to pursue; blessed are the rich and with great honor all over the world.

He was telling believers that there is a certain requirement if people want to receive the blessings of the Lord's kingdom. Christian believers must be in control of God's guide, by God's ways and values, which were laid down in the Scripture and not by the ways and values of this world of sin.

First, God's requirement is to be poor in Spirit. We must recognize that we are not spiritually self-sufficient; we need the Holy Spirit's life, power and spirit sustaining grace in order to inherit the kingdom of God. No amount of wealth and riches can buy the kingdom of God.

Jesus Christ gave us the parable that is also applied to the rich people of this earth, "For I was hungry and you gave me something to eat, I was thirsty and you gave me something to drink, I was a stranger and you invited me in, I needed clothes and you clothed me, I was sick and you came to visit me. Then the righteous will answer him, Lord, when did we see you hungry and feed. The King will reply, I tell you the truth, whatever you did for one of the least of these brothers of famine, you did for me" (Matthew 25:35-40). Jesus Christ said, "For I was hungry you did not feed me, and he said that if you did not feed the hungry among you; you did not feed me, if you did not visit those who are sick in the hospital, in prison you did not visit me." Christ wants us to care for our fellow citizens. He is telling us that any good word that we did merits the happiness of heaven; even though at his coming he will judge the world of sin, by the same rule by which he governs it. He will, therefore, reward those who have been obedient Christians, upon God's promise, which was purchased by the precious blood of Jesus Christ.

It is the promise and purchase that most important obedience is on the qualification of the person. God work of charity to the poor and teaches believers general faith that works by love is all in all Christianity. Christians must deny themselves of all the things of this world; they must be content and cheerfully read to help the poor and the needy. Christians must love their brothers and sisters in Christ. They must give proof of their love by always readying to do good; communicate with care for each other. Believers must show their love for the poor for Christ's sake, out of their love for him; their good deeds will be accepted, which are done in the name of Jesus Christ. Those who put on Jesus Christ have clothes to keep them warm. For those who have healthful souls, those who are sick and for those who are in prison, Jesus Christ has set them free. The work of love and beneficence, according to our ability, are necessary to salvation. Those characters must be the proofs of our love, as well as our professed subjection to the gospel of Christ. Consequently, those who show no mercy for the poor and the needy shall have judgment without mercy.

With this in mind, the rich must be willing and ready to help the poor in any way possible. "Jesus answered if you want to be perfect, go, sell your possessions and give to the poor and you will have treasure in heaven. Then come, follow me" (Matthew 19:21-22). The young ruler came short of his love of the world and the lust of it; Christ tried him by telling him, "Jesus said unto him, if though wilt be perfect, go and sell that thou, hast." Jesus let him know that boasting about his obedience on keeping the law. Jesus Christ is telling us the same thing today, that if we would approve ourselves as Christians in deed and would be found at last the heirs of the inheritance of eternal life, we must set our minds practically on Him. Prefer the heavenly treasures before all the wealth and riches of this world. Jesus Christ is telling us that we must dispose of what we have in this world and honor God and his service. Sell all we have and give it to the poor. For example, giving alms is necessary; it is evidence of the contempt of the world and compassion to our brothers and sisters. When we give our life to Christ, we must let go of all the world's lust because we cannot serve two masters.

Christ knew that the young rulers have a covetousness sin that beset in, even though he got them honestly. Yet, he was unable to part with his wealth; by doing so, he automatically discovered his insincerity. We Christians must depend upon our hope for an abundant recompense for all we left behind to Christ in this universe. Christians must trust God for our happiness out of sight, which will make us spiritually rich and make amends for all our expenses in God's service. Jesus Christ's assurance of a treasure in heaven is more than sufficient. Jesus promises make his precepts easy, and his yoke very pleasant, sweet and comfortable. Christians must devote themselves entirely, solely for the character and control of our Lord Jesus Christ. Strictly conform to his image and pattern. Keep his laws from the heart of our love for him, as well as our dependence on him, and with a holy competence of everything else in comparison of him. Christians must sell all that they have, give to the poor and follow Jesus Christ our redeemer King. The Scripture said, "If I give all my goods to feed the poor, and have not love, it profits me nothing." The young ruler went away sorrowful because he was a rich man, and he loved his riches. Therefore, he was unable to follow Christ; he went away.

Biblically, those who have much wealth in this world are the greatest temptation of love for their wealth. The love and lust of this world keep so many people away from Jesus Christ to a great hindrance in the way to heaven. Many Christians today were ruined by sins they committed, which they do not want to part with, or are feeling reluctant to do away with; they leave Jesus Christ sorrowfully and never truly sorrow for leaving him, because if they feels sorry, they might denounce the sin, and return to him.

When the young man heard this, he went away sad because he had great wealth. Our Lord and Savior Jesus Christ tested the heart of the young rich man in the area of his greatest weakness, which is his wealth that he trusts and hangs onto. He was not willing to put Jesus Christ before and above his possessions. What our Lord Jesus was telling the young rich man is that he must care for the needs of others; he must be willing to give up anything that is not of God or what is not pleasing to God in his life. He must be committed to Christ alone and him only to worship, not to worship his riches.

Where justice is denied, where poverty is enforced, where ignorance prevails, and where any one class is made to feel that society is an organized conspiracy to oppress, rob and degrade them, neither persons nor property will be safe.

—Frederick Douglass

CHAPTER TEN
Are You Sure The Rich Want To Redistribute Wealth?

Some rich people do not want to redistribute their wealth because they say that they work hard for their wealth while some of the poor people are very lazy; they do not want to do anything with their lives. Some rich people believe that poor people put themselves in that position. Whereby, some rich people believe that it is the government's problem to care for the poor and the needy and medical care for the people in their country.

For some rich people, not only do they not want to redistribute wealth, they don't even want to pay taxes or their correct taxes to the government of their country. Giving and charity to the poor is a foundational principle in every nation, especially in nations of extreme poverty. The people who were blessed with financial stability should or must help those who do not have enough to eat. Rich people must be willing to contribute through charitable organizations or directly to the poor on their own.

Some rich people want to redistribute wealth because they are more successful than other people or far more better in what they do, or they are better than the poor by making wise choices. They sometime might be thinking that they work harder and that is why they are very successful. Some rich people do not want to redistribute wealth because they feel that the poor are far below in poverty because of how they put themselves below other people in their country. Either by income earning or maintaining good health by staying away from any lifestyle that can give them medical problems.

All these are the excuses given by the rich to justify why they do not want to redistribute their wealth or help the poor. Some of them believe that poverty is the act of God. Therefore, the rich do not want to help the poor because they believe the poor have been destined to be poor on earth and those who are rich have been destined to be rich on earth. Some rich people do not even want to give money to their kids; some do not even want to leave their kids plenty of money because they believe that their kids should work and make their own money. They might also be scared that leaving plenty of money for their kids might cause them problems, or shorten their life or ruin their reputation. They believe that inheritance is a bad habit for their kids. The rich people feel that they do not have any obligation to give to the poor, but they can do so if they feel like it.

All around the world, the rich do not realize that poverty could result in a crime. Therefore, the rich in that community are not saved. Rich people know that children are born into poverty in poor nations of extreme poverty. They believe the world did not provide for everyone. Some people have good education, some don't, but the rich need to help the poor in every way, in any circumstance in any nation where people are in need of help without giving any excuses.

The homeless need homes and stable lives. The rich must be able to offer help. Build houses for the homeless voluntarily and willingly so that the homeless have a place to sleep. People believe that the government body of every country in the world causes the people to be poor. Therefore, rich people believe that the political government must make a good plan and implement the plan for a structure that will eradicate poverty in their country.

All the rich wealthy people in the world should help the poor in all the areas of their lives. Medical problems will be reduced; the rich people should help the children of poverty in another country, where children are dying of hunger every day. The rich do not trust some charitable organizations because they don't give to the poor or spend the money for the poor. Instead, they make themselves rich while the poor die of lack of food, shelter and clean water in all the nations.

The rich love in their hearts to brag over poor people and they turned them away from getting relief; they also threatened them and forced them to abscond, especially the poor children who were fatherless. They also made them motherless after they have taken away their father's life. They broke the mother's heart, starve the children and leave them to die. People like this forget about the judgment of God; they show no mercy to the poor and they shall not receive mercy from God.

Grant me the treasure of sublime poverty: permit the distinctive sign of our order to be that it does not possess anything of its own beneath the sun, for the glory of your name, and that it have no other patrimony than begging.

—Francis of Assisi

CHAPTER ELEVEN
What Is The Reward For The Rich?

Our Lord Jesus Christ teaches that the poor are always going to be with us. Poverty and need are not supposed to be permanent conditions of people. It should be temporary if everyone around them works together and change their living condition in any way possible that can bring this change to them. Poverty is a phenomenon where, if all the people including the government work hard, it will go away from the community, country and from individual families.

The responsibility of Christians is to be generous and provide for their needs to the best of their ability until the end of the world when Christ returns. Christians will always be called by God to help the poor (1st Corinthians 13:3). Christian life must be a life of love. A life of great miraculous faith that can move mountains is a great faith of an accomplishment as well as achievement in the life of men; but love in God's account is more important than faith.

Love is more than the faith in the world. Saving faith is never to be compared or in conjunction with love. Also, the faith of miracles, the outward actions of love where there is no liberal and love from the heart is unprofitable. If we give away all our belongings to feed the poor but at the same time we withhold the heart of love from God, it profits us nothing; the Scripture is saying that even if we go through long suffering and sacrifice our lives for the faith of the gospel, this will stand us in no stead without love. True love is from the very heart and spirit of our gospel religion. Love is the bond of true life in Christ and the meaning of the Gospel of God to all the people in all the nations.

"And do not forget to do good and to share with others, for with such sacrifices God is pleased" (Hebrews, 13:16). Christians must bring their sacrifices to the altar, the sacrifices of praise to God, which we must offer up to the Lord continually, which included our adoration and prayers and our thanksgiving; all sacrifices of all misdeeds and Christian love, not contending ourselves to offer the sacrifices of our lips, words, but the fruit of our lips gives praise to the Lord and increases in sacrifice of our good deeds.

When rich people give from their hearts, it pleases God. God, in turn, blesses them more and more without measure. For example if the rich give freely to the poor, is like when musicians come to Central Park in New York City and give a free concert. All the poor people who have no money to buy ticket to go to the concert will sleep in Central Park overnight in order to get a place, in order to get a closer place to the concert. This act of the musicians remembering the poor makes God happy and he always blesses them.

Another example is the footballers during the beginning of every school year. They will load book bags, notebooks and all other school items from K-grade to high school, and go from neighborhood to neighborhood distributing all the school materials to the kids. This act of kindness will bring great reward to the athletic person in so many ways that he or she cannot imagine. On one occasion, parents asked one of the footballers, "How do you have time to remember us?" The Athletic person answered, "There is no time that I forget about you. And giving to the little children, helping in the area of their education always makes me very happy throughout the year."

This shows clearly that the reward of giving is always great. "Better a poor man whose walk is blameless than a fool whose lips are perverse—wealth brings many friends, but a poor man's friend deserts him" (Proverbs, 19:1, 4). These proverbs are telling us that there are a lot of friends who called themselves our friends but they were superficial friends attracted to our wealth or they called themselves friends because they wanted to use us for their own gain. They were attracted to the wealth of people. Flies are drawn to the honey and honey bees, while a poor person has few friends because he or she cannot provide for anyone.

Believers must be careful with people who are fake and artificial friends. "A generous man will prosper; he who refreshes others will himself be refreshed" (Proverbs 11:25). God the Father Almighty promises that those who give generously will receive back more than they give. Our Lord Jesus Christ blesses those who are kind and generous with his loving kindness, whether it is in their financial giving or in giving of themselves by making themselves available to help others who are in need of their help.

New testament studies explain clearly and in a precise manner teach that we are the stewards of God's gifts and we must use them for his glory and for the benefit of those who are in need. He who is rich and wise must freely and willingly influence people for righteousness. Believers should lead people to Jesus Christ, salvation and lives of righteousness. Christian believers who are rich in the rivers of the grace of God are exhorts to excel in giving to the church, the poor and the needy, both fellow believers and unbelievers.

As long as we belong to the Lord, whatever we have on this earth is not our own. It belongs to him and it is for his glory. We must have total love and trust for our Lord. We must be determined in our hearts to serve the Lord with all our possessions. When we give to those who are in need, we store up a treasure in heaven and we give to enhance and advance the kingdom of God. Giving will be seen as proof of our love for our Lord and Savior, and it should be done cheerfully, sacrificially, willingly and voluntarily. The reward is great because we will find out that by giving to God and giving to the poor we are sowing not only money. We are sowing faith, our time, and our services. Therefore, the reward is greater faith and blessing. When God supplies us abundantly, it is because he wants us to multiply our efforts in doing good to others in our work or service for him. Giving to the poor helps us to increase our dedication to God, our focus on God, increases our devotion to God, helps us to work harder so that we can be able to be in a position to give more and more. Giving also activates the work of the kingdom of God in our financial services and spending.

The rewards of giving physically, spiritually, financially to God and to those who are suffering are incomparable. "He who oppresses the poor shows contempt for their maker, but whoever is kind to the needy honors God" (Proverbs, 14:31). People of this world's character and condition are measured by their behavior toward the poor among them in the neighborhood. God said he who has mercy on the poor and the needy are ready to do good in the Lord's eyes and does do all that which is pleasing to Him.

God is telling us that whoever should mistreat or whoever should take advantage of a poor person offends God and shows contempt for him. The poor are also made and created in God's image and they are the objects of his special mercy and concern. Therefore, the gospel of God must be preached to the poor and to the rich. "A generous man will himself be blessed for he shares his food with the poor" (Proverbs, 22:9). God, always in his pleasure, blesses the rich who give to the poor, and he blesses their business, their children, and their entire family and relatives.

"The righteous care about justice for the poor, but the wicked has no such concern" (Proverbs 29:7). It is the duty of humanity to consider the poor and the needy among them. The judgment of the poor must be considered by those who sit in judgment.

Concern for the poor and the needy were brought to the attention of the Israelites in the Old Testament, as one of God's important standards of righteousness. Today, true followers of Jesus Christ must do likewise, be able to share their concerns about the suffering, the poor and afflicted that they should be treated fairly and compassionately. They also must be made known that they have the same opportunity to hear the gospel in their own language.

They have the opportunity to respond to the teaching of the gospel of the kingdom of God that will come to them with many blessings in so many ways and in various ways at any time. Apostle Paul said, "Remember this: Whoever sows sparingly will also reap sparingly, and whoever sows generously will also reap generously. Each man should give what he has decided in his heart to give, not reluctantly or under compulsion, for God loves a cheerful giver. And God is able to make all grace abound to you, so that in all things at all times, having all that you need, you will abound in every good work" (2nd Corinthians 9:6-8). The grace of our Lord Jesus Christ's Scripture says; though Jesus Christ was rich, and yet for our sake he became poor; that we might be made rich, rich in the love of God. Jesus Christ our Savior Lord, Christ was rich in the blessings of the new covenant, rich in the hope of eternal life. Christians must love the poor out of what they have given to help the poor, as we live our lives upon the love of Jesus Christ our Lord.

Our Lord and Savior urged all the believers through Apostle Paul that Christians must give either generously, not sparingly. God will reward them accordingly.

In the book of Matthew, our Lord said, "Do not judge, or you too will be judged, for in the same way you judge others, you will be judged, and with the measure you use, it will be measured to you" (Matthew 7:1-2). Our Lord and Savior was teaching us in this scripture not to judge others. We must judge our own character but we must not judge our brothers and sisters. Christians must not judge rashly. We must not judge uncharitably, unmercifully, or with the motive of revenge, and with a desire not to hurt others. Christians must not judge through the hearts of others, nor their intentions, for it is God's prerogative to try to judge the heart of man. We must not judge their eternal state, nor call them be little names. Words that can demean others must not come out of believing Christians; Christians must always be ready to counsel, comfort and help those who are in need, but not to judge them. The reason for this is that we ourselves will not be judged. No mercy shall be shown to the reputation of those who show no mercy to the reputation of others. If God judges those who judge, they will receive a greater condemnation; if we rather judge ourselves, we shall not be judges of the Lord because God will forgive those who forgive others.

Our Lord was telling us that as a Christian we must not engage in the habit of criticizing others while ignoring our own faults. Believers must first submit themselves to God's righteous standard before attempting to examine and influence the conduct of other Christians. In the same way, we must not condemn those who give sparingly. Giving is not a loss, but it is a form of savings; it results in substantial benefits for those who give. Whereby, the apostle was concentrated primarily on the quality of our hearts in our giving, not the quantity of what we give without coming from our hearts; our giving must be commensurable with our hearts' desire for giving and our motives for giving.

We have to remember the widow in the synagogue who gave a little that she had, but God considered it much because of the proportion she gave and her complete dedication. When the believers and the rich gave all that they can give to help those in need, they find out that God's grace will provide sufficiently for their own needs, and even more, that they will abound in every good work, in all the areas of their business and in their position.

To receive the reward of giving the hearts of the giver must be made rich in sincere love and compassion for others. Giving of ourselves and our possessions results in supplying the needs of poor brothers and sisters, praise and thanksgiving to God. Reciprocal to love from those who receive our help, the rich will receive a great reward of love from God and from the poor and the needy.

Our life of poverty is as necessary as the work itself. Only in heaven will we see how much we owe to the poor for helping us to love God better because of them. Loneliness and the feeling of being unwanted is the most terrible poverty.

—Mother Teresa

CHAPTER TWELVE
What Happens To Both The Rich And The Poor In The End?

The rich and the poor will rejoice in the Lord at the end of their lives. The poor, the needy and the rich will clearly know that God is the one and only who acts and does in their lives for his good pleasure. The Scripture revealed in the Old Testament what God the Almighty said, "If there is a poor man among your brothers in any of the towns of the land that the Lord your God is giving you, do not be hard hearted or tightfisted towards your poor brothers. Rather be opening handed and freely lend him whatever he needs. There will always be poor people in the land. Therefore I command you to open handed towards your brother and towards the poor and the needy in your land" (Deuteronomy 15:7-8, 11).

We have to see that believers and the rich people of the earth are taking care of the poor among us is one of the commands of God Almighty. Those who are rich are commanded by God to care for the poor and the needy because the poor, the suffering, the needy, the wealthy and rich people are all the same in the heart of God. God created the poor and the rich, and He wants us to care for each other in any circumstances.

God's love was expected to grow out of a sincere desire to obey God by helping the poor and the suffering.

We must use our material possessions to help those who have real needs such as medical needs, financial needs, food needs, water needs and clothing needs. If we are selfish and do not care for the needs of others among us we cut ourselves short of the blessings of God. Especially the needs of those who are sick with HIV/AID and diverse diseases. Our Lord made greater emphasis to us for the need and our compassion, empathy and kindness toward those who have suffered in some areas of their lives or those who experience problems in so many circumstances that brought poverty or sickness to their lives.

By caring for the poor, it will make all of us appreciate the love of God and we will in turn love ourselves to the point that at the end we will see clearly that God is the one who gives us all things to enjoy on this earth. The Scripture says, "Blessed is he who has regard for the weak; the Lord delivers him in times of trouble, the Lord will protect him and preserve his life; he will bless him in the land and not surrender him to the desire of his foes" (Psalm 41:1-2). Christian believers must know that heavens, heavens only, are the Lord's and the earth, an inconsiderable part of the creation, has been neglected with no interest in it, but the earth and everything that dwells in it is the Lord's.

God gave the earth to the children of men, but He still reserved to himself the property. People of this earth are just his tenants. The gold, mines, fruits, produce, all the animals in the forest and cattle on the mountains, land and houses all the great improvements that happen on this earth, are with the knowledge of God the skills and industry of man and all are from Him, and belong to Him. This earth is full of God's riches; the entire world belongs to the Lord. God made the earth and filled it for the use of man because God made the earth out of nothing; he formed it and made it according to his eternal counsels and according to his own knowledge, of his own mind. God in his mercy established the earth, fixed it in a way that when one generation passes another generation will come. More importantly, God's providence continued and never failed in all his creation. He provided for the poor and the needy in so many ways during many time.

Both the rich and the poor will be blessed according to the will of God. God has a special concern for the weak, the distressed and the helpless. In his mercy, he blesses those who show loving kindness to the needy because our Lord said, "Blessed are the merciful, for they will be shown mercy" (Matthew 5:7).

Blessed are the merciful because our Lord and Savior pronounced the merciful blessed because God accepts the willing mind. Christians must patiently bear our own afflictions and the afflictions of others. Christians must sympathize and partake of the afflictions of their brother; they must show pity. Bowels of mercy must be put on by Christians at all times. Christians must also have compassion on the souls in the heaven of heaven. The happiness of those seen, God is a promise to those, and those only who are pure in heart. Christians must give thanks to God because the pure in heart are capable of seeing the vision of a Holy God; all that are pure in heart, are truly sanctified, all their desires are nothing else but what the sight of God will satisfy. The Scripture said the peacemakers are happy. The wisdom that is from above is always first pure and then peaceable. The blessed ones are pure toward God. They love others and they desire and delight in peace. Christians must try their best anywhere they are to preserve the peace industriously and to recover it when it is broken.

The peacemaker is working hand-in-hand together with our Lord who came into this world to proclaim peace on earth. The peacemakers shall always be called the children of God; the peacemaker will always be blessed. The same way those who are persecuted for righteousness' sake are very happy. Christians who are persecuted, hunted, pursued, imprisoned or rundown, they look for them to destroy them. They are abandoned and people plan all manner of evil against them falsely. They suffer for righteousness' sake. They are blessed, for it is an honor to them. It is an opportunity of glorifying Christ and experiencing special comforts of his presence; they shall be rewarded in heaven.

Because the merciful are full of compassion and pity, those who are afflicted and who are suffering either from sin or earthly sorrow. The merciful always work hard to reduce the suffering of people among them by bringing them to the grace and the help of God through our Lord and Savior Jesus Christ. When the rich and believers are showing mercy to the poor and the needy, the Lord will look down from heaven and fill them with his mercy. The Lord will show mercy to both of them at the end; both of them will receive mercy of the Lord. The rich shared God's compassion for those who are in need. The rich can be able to pray confidently, boldly that the Lord will deliver them when they are in trouble to protect them from all harm, to bless their lives. They will pray with confidence that the Lord destroyed the power of Satan and the power of the enemies, as well as for the Lord's full presence to be upon them, the healing power when they are experiencing any sickness in their body.

The Scripture says, "The earth is the Lord's, and everything in it, the world, and all who live in it; for he founded it upon the seas and established it upon the waters" (Psalm 24:1-2). David said blessed is he who remembers the poor and provides for their relief, and therefore was sure God would, according to his promise, strengthened and comfort them in sickness. The Scripture said, "Blessed are the merciful, for they shall obtain mercy—the mercy which is required from individuals who come to the world; the mercy which will make us to consider the poor, the need and the afflicted in mind, soul and body." We must sympathize with them and make a charitable contribution for them. He or she who considers the poor shall be richly blessed on earth. Having mercy for the poor is the godliness that was the promise of life that is now and forever with blessings unspeakable.

Both the rich and the poor are enjoying the love of God because he owns the earth, the sea, and everything that dwells in it. He commanded the rain to fall, the snow to fall, the sun to rise at its proper time and the moon to shine at its time. Nothing is beyond his reach; nothing is impossible for him to do in heaven and on this earth. His promises will be fulfilled for the rich and the poor.

The end of both the rich and the poor is the eternal life, which God provided for all the people of this earth, if they come to him in humble obedience. In Jesus Christ, there is no East, no West, no North and no South. In Christ, there is no poor and no rich. We are all the children of God from this earth to heaven and we must care for each other's needs with the love of God, which is in Christ Jesus our Lord. Christ wants all those who believed in him to worship and serve God and he wants them to receive his blessings and we must be able to pursue a righteous life with pure hearts, which is the inner holiness.

There are four billion cell phones in use today. Many of them are in the hands of market vendors, rickshaw drivers, and others who've historically lacked access to education and opportunity. Information networks have become a great leveler, and we should use them together to help lift people out of poverty and give them a freedom from want.

—Hillary Clinton

SUMMARY

The world's poorest countries are poorer because of HIV/AIDS, malaria, tuberculosis, hunger, lack of clean water and sustainable energy conservation; all these problems are expected to triple by the year 2030: 1.2 million to 3.6 million per year. Road accidents will soon be the number five cause of death in poor countries. These countries only account for half of the world traffic. In those countries, 10% of traffic disasters occurred. This is one of the problems that is costing the people their lives.

In the nation of Nigeria, there are 33.7 deaths per 100,000 people. In the nation of Pakistan, death by motorcycle is 90% for not wearing a helmet. In the nation of Jamaica, it is 6% because they wear helmets. In the nation of Russia, the fatality rate is higher than other European countries. Kenyan minibus deaths are higher at 38%. In the nation of China, 200 million buses are on the road; there are 24 fatalities per 100,000 people. African nations have the world's most dangerous roads.

Poverty varies from country to country. Between 1981-2008, people in the developing countries live on less than $1.25 a day. Over one billion people around the world remain in need. Some government operations wasted the country's money; corruption, and conflict waste public resources and they discourage foreign investors. Poverty needs must be confronted and dealt with.

During his inaugural ceremony January 20, 1961, John F. Kennedy United State President warned, "If a free society cannot help the many who are poor, it cannot save the few who are rich" (January 20, 1961).

In the case of Hoffman versus South African Airways; Justice Ngcobo of the Constitutional Court of South Africa stated, "Our constitution protect the weak, the marginalize, the socially outcast and the victims of prejudice and stereotyping. It is only when these groups are protected that we can be secured that our own rights are protected" (2001 CHR 329 at 354).

God Almighty Father of all mercies and creator of all things who created the poor and the needy, the rich and the wealthy of the people in the world, want us to help each other. From the Old Testament to the New Testament, God commanded the rich to help the poor. This is how we can love each other, show the act of kindness of our Lord to each other, and share the wealth of the earth, which no money can buy, which is the love of God in Christ Jesus our Lord.

The Scripture revealed, "Religion that God our Father accepts as pure and faultless is this; to look after orphans and widows in their distress and to keep oneself from being polluted by the world" (James 1:27). Apostle James gives two principles that define the content of true and pure religion. Christian believers and the rich, those who are in authority, must have genuine devotion to God in all the areas of their lives.

They must have love for the people who are in need, such as the orphans, the widows and people who cannot support themselves; people who have no guardian or helper. The rich and the believers are expected to show them the same care that God shows toward the fatherless and widows. Today in our society, there are millions of people in this world who are in need, who are homeless, who lack medical care for their children; whereas some rich are spending millions of dollars on their pets, leaving twelve million dollars in inheritance for their dogs, spending millions on a play station at their home, when they hardly live there. The rich must try to have compassion toward the needy and those who are suffering.

They need the blessing from the most high God in all the areas of their lives. They might not lack money, but they will still be in need of something in their lives. Among Christian brothers and sisters in Christ, there are those who are in need of loving care and they should seek to alleviate their distress by showing them that God cares for them. A holy life is when we show our love for others and accompany it by a love for God expressed in separation from the world's sinful ways. Love for others must be combined with holiness before the Almighty God. We must know that nothing we acquire on this earth can go to heaven with us; they are material things of the world, which stay in the world after we have gone.

The Scripture revealed, "Every good and perfect gift is from above, coming down from the Father of the heavenly lights, who does not change like shifting shadows. He chose to give us birth through the word of truth that we might be a kind of first fruits of all he created" (James 1:17-18). God never changes; our changes are caused by ourselves. The Father of light in whom there is no variability never turns from one way to another way. Jesus Christ is the same yesterday, today and forever. Every good gift is from the Father of light. He gives the light of reasoning, the light of learning, the light of his divine revelation, which is from above. Everything we received on this earth is from the Father. Christian regeneration and all holy, happy, honors must be ascribed to our Lord and Savior. A true Christian is a creature begotten anew. It is of God's own will, not by our skill or our power but purely from the good will and from the grace of God. The gospel is indeed the word of truth and it produces life everlasting.

As we give here on earth to those who are in need, the sick, the poor the Father of heavenly light is always happy to give us all things that we need and even things that we don't need. Father sees and knows; he is the immortal, the invisible, the only wise God. All knowing, all powerful, all merciful and mighty God, the one and only, the Ancient of days, the ever living Lord our Savior.

The more we give to the poor and the needy, the more He blesses us. He will open the gates of heaven and shower us his blessings immeasurable, abundantly, amazingly more than we can imagine in our lives. He is the channel of blessings.

God made us for each other for us to care for each other in any earthly circumstances. The Scripture reveals, "All the believers were one in heart and mind. No one claimed that any of his possessions was his own, but they shared everything they had" (Acts 4:32). The multitude of those who believed were of one heart, and one soul—even in Jerusalem converted Christians in thousands who were added to the church daily, many, many in different ages and conditions they have one faith in the Lord and join the Lord in holy love. They were blessed fruits of Jesus Christ's dying order and command to his disciples. They must love one another and his prayer for them as well as they may be one. Christ is telling us today that we must be one in him and love one another, that the church must be one. All for the Lord's glory and the beauty of the Lord, our God shone upon the apostles and upon us today.

Christians were receiving the outpouring of abundant grace in all that they said and have done. Every experience, even though they were poor including children, they did not take away the poverty; they were indifferent to it. They did not call what they have their own. They distribute it willingly, put down their estate and other property. They forsake all for Christ and for others to help fellow Christians because there are many poor among them who received the gospel and there were many rich Christians who were able to care for the poor Christians. Therefore, food and clothing were distributed according to everyone's need.

During early Christianity, the apostles shared everything they owned and used it for the work of the Lord. No one claimed that they owned anything for themselves. This is the act of God that our Lord requires because they were able to care for the needy and the poor among them, especially the widows.

They were able to support the orphan children who have no mother and father through diseases and plague that trouble the world. The apostolic era was so good and pleasant. There were no rich and no poor among them; all were equal. Today in our society if we can have the same treatment for each individual the world would be a better place to live. Crime violence and hatred will be reduced and poverty will be eradicated. Our Lord said during his teaching "Then Jesus said to his host, when you give a luncheon or dinner, do not invite your friends, your brothers or relatives, or your rich neighbors; if you do, they may invite you back and so you will be repaid. However, when you give banquet, invite the poor, the crippled, the lame, the blind, and you will be blessed. Although they cannot repay you, you will be repay at the resurrection of the righteous" (Luke 14:12).

Christ said when you make a feast invite not thy friends, and brothers and neighbors who are rich. He said that one feast for the rich will make a great many meals for the poor. Be forward to help the poor when you make a feast. Invite the poor when you make a feast. Invite the poor, the restless and maimed, those who have nothing to live upon, and those who are unable to work for a living. This is the object of charity. They want necessities; furnish them, and they will recompense you with their prayers. They will eat and go away and thank God for you. Christians should know that not all the work of love may be rewarded on this earth, for the things of this world are not the best, but they shall not lose their reward.

Our Lord and Savior teaches and warns that those who exalt themselves in this life will be put to shame in the future kingdom of heaven; Christ explained clearly that what is more important than earthly honor is our place of honor before God. Such honor cannot be secured by self-assertiveness, for it comes only through humility and through servanthood by seeking the praise that comes from the only God.

POVERTY QUOTES

Poverty is a veil that obscures the face of greatness. An appeal is a mask covering the face of tribulation.
—Khalil Gibran

Do not waste your time on social questions. What is the matter with the poor is poverty; what is the matter with the rich is uselessness.
—George Bernard Shaw

There are many people in South Africa who are rich and who can share those riches with those not so fortunate who have not been able to conquer poverty.
—Nelson Mandela

Poverty is the mother of crime.
—Marcus Aurelius

The community which has neither poverty nor riches will always have the noblest principles.
—Plato

Resolve not to be poor: whatever you have, spend less. Poverty is a great enemy to human happiness; it certainly destroys liberty, and it makes some virtues impracticable, and others extremely difficult.

—Samuel Johnson

The down-to-earth Pope called for greater austerity from religious figures last week, saying, "It hurts me when I see a priest or non with the latest-model car. You can't to this. A car is necessary to do a lot of work, but, please, choose a more humble one. If you like the fancy one, just think about how many children are dying of hunger in the world.

—Pope Francis

Take care of God's creation. But above all, take care of people in need.

—Pope Francis

The secret of Christian living is love. Only love fills the empty spaces caused by evil.

—Pope Francis

The fight against evil is long and difficult. It is essential to pray constantly and to be patient.

—Pope Francis

God is everywhere: We have to know how to find him in order to be able to proclaim Him in the language of each and every culture; every reality, every language, has its own rhythm.

—Pope Francis

I have a dogmatic certainty: God is in every person's life. God is in everyone's life. Even if the life of a person has been a disaster, even if it is destroyed by vices, drugs or anything else – God is in this person's life. You can, you must try to seek God in every human life.

—Pope Francis

PRAYER FOR THE POVERTY OF THE NATIONS

Lord God Almighty, Father Son and Holy Spirit, you are the immortal the invisible, the only wise God who created the poor and the rich. I pray that all the people in the nations will go out into the caves and villages of this world in peace and great courage to help those who are in need in various ways. I pray that people of this earth should learn how to hold on to what is good and stop returning evil for evil. If any group of people or any one needs help in any city or neighborhood, they should help them in our society.

Lord Jesus Christ, help us to strengthen the fainthearted; teach us how to support the weak; help those who are suffering among us. Help us to honor all the people without prejudice, either rich, or poor, adult, or children, men or women. Everyone on this earth deserves to be honored, not only the rich people. Our Lord and Savior let love, the love of God in Christ Jesus, prevail. Let the people of the earth, all the inhabitant of this earth, love you O' Lord and help us to serve you with the spirit of rejoicing in the power of the Holy Spirit.

Lord Jesus Christ, with your love and help we will be what you want us to be. Lord Jesus Christ, send food to those little children who are dying because of lack of food. Send medical Doctors physicians to those children who are in need of medical care around the world. Send help to those children who are in orphanage homes and foster homes around the world. Touch the hearts and the minds of those who are in government, to continue to make all efforts in order to reduce poverty in their nation. Let the government officials work hard to make sure that water and sustainable energy, clean water reaches those villages and towns in their country where they are in need of clean water to drink.

Be the suppliers of clean water in the rural areas of the world. I pray for rain on all the crops for the farmers and more help where there is civil war and international war, where the people are dying because of the chemical weapons that they are using against each other. Lord God Almighty let your blessings of your Son, and the Holy Spirit is upon every living soul on this earth and under the earth and let your blessings remain on them forever.

Lord Jesus Christ, let your light shine in this world, let your glory fill the sky, let your joy fill the hearts and minds of everyone in every nation of this earth. Continue by working through the United Nations in order to bring hunger to the end and everyone to have food to eat in their country in abundance. Everyone have clean water, sustainable energy, education for the children, and every one receives proper medical care at all times. Lord Jesus Christ, you said we should remember the poor among us always; touch the minds and hearts of the people who have plenty and those who does not have at all to help each other. Lord, show us, teach us, help us what to do in order to remember the poor. Help us to remember that what we do for the poor and the needy we do it for you. In your matchless, great holy name I pray; accept my prayers, Amen, amen, amen.

In poverty and other misfortunes of life, true friends are a sure refuge. The young they keep out of mischief; to the old they are a comfort and aid in their weakness, and those in the prime of life they incite to noble deeds.

—Aristotle

BIBLICAL INDEX

BIBLIOGRAPHY

World Bible Dictionary Student Edition by Don Fleming World Bible Publishers 1996

The Dead Sea Scrolls—Introduction to Biblical Archaeology November 1, 1997 Rose Publishing

NIV Archaeological Study Bible: An Illustrated Walk through Biblical History and Culture by Walter c. Kaiser Jr. and Duane Garrett Zondervan Feb 25, 2006

The Bible as History by Werner Keller Bantam—Publisher Nov.1, 1983

Expository Dictionary of Bible Words by Stephen D. Renn Hendrickson Publishers 2005

Easton's Bible Dictionary by Matthew George Packard Technologies—Publisher (March 18, 2009)

Believer's Bible Commentary, William MacDonald Edited By Arthur Farstad, 1995 Thomas Nelson Publishers Nashville Atlanta, USA (1995).

Evangelical Dictionary of Biblical Theology, Edited by Walter A. Elwell, 1996 by Baker Book House Company Grand Rapids, Michigan, USA (1996).

The Holy Bible, In King James Version, Dugan Publishers, Inc., 1987 Gordonsville, Tennessee Printed in Colombia (1987).

The Student Bible, New Revised Standard Version1994 by The Zondervan Corporation Published by Zondervan Grand Rapids, Michigan, USA (1994)

National Center for Biotechnology Information U. S. Library of Medicine 8600 Rockville Pike, Bethsaida MD, 20894 USA

List of Constitutional Judgment of the Constitutional count of South Africa delivered 2000, 28, Sept. 2000—Human Right and human Dignity Fair labor Practices Appealed Constitutional Court SA 628; 2001 8/28/2000 Judgment.

The Eritrean Struggle for Independence: Domination, Resistance, Nationalism, 1941-1993. Cambridge University Press. Keen, David 2005

Conflict and Collision in Sierra Leone Oxford: James Carrey Publisher: International Book Marketing Service ltd Published 9/18/2012—Ebola Virus Disease by Terrence James Victorino—Editor

Ebola Virus, Bundibugyo Virus, Sudan Virus, Tai forest Virus, Viral hemorrhagic fever. Edwin Michael Bridges 1990 Northern Asia. World geomorphology. Cambridge University Press pp.—124-126.

State of Food Insecurity in the World, 2008 FAO Food Security Statistics

State of Poverty in Europe 90-2007 World Bank View shared Report ID-1336

UNDP Human Development Report 2009 Table#3: Human Poverty Development Countries. UNICEF—Poverty in South America March 27, 2013

IFAD Strategy for Rural Poverty Reduction in Latin America and the Caribbean. International Fund for Agricultural Development

The Long Struggle of Entrea for Independence and Constructive Peace Spokesman Press Iyob, Ruth 1997 Berkley: university of California Press, 687 pp. Cliff, Lionel & Davidson, Basil (1988)

Deaton, Angus Understanding Consumption, Oxford University Press (1992)

Friedman, Jonathan Consumption and Identity Studies in Anthropology and History Washington DC Taylor & Francis (1994)

Basic Needs in Development Planning—Michael Hopkins and Rolp Vardar Hoevan Gouver, Aldersot, UK, 1983

Poverty in Canada: Implications for health and quality of life by Dennis Raphael forward by Rob Rainer and Jack Layton (1st Edition Comedian Scholars Press April 13, 2007

UN—OHRLLS list of least Developed Countries URL accessed June 7, 2006

Poverty and population in Lagos People & the planet URL accessed June 7, 2006 by Okunlola, Paul June 24, 2002 Watts, M, 1983 Silent, Violence Food Famine and peasantry in Northern Nigeria.

BOOKS PREVIOUSLY PUBLISHED
BY THE AUTHOR
Grace Dola Balogun by Grace Religious Books
Publishing & Distributors, Inc. New York

CHRIST'S LIFE IN THE LIFE OF CHRISTIANS

This book will help you to understand your position in Jesus Christ as a Christian. Reading this book will also give clear understanding of who Christ is in the life of believing Christians. It will give you more divine ability as well as the power of the indwelling of the Holy Spirit that Christ gave to all who believe and gave their life to him. Jesus Christ is the one who initiates and the one who establishes the new covenant and his heavenly ministry is far beyond and far more superior to the ministry of Old Testament priests. The new covenant is an agreement, promise, the last will and testament and a statement of intention to be bestow divine grace and blessing on all those who believe in God; those who in sincere repentance and through faith accept Jesus Christ as the true Son of God; those who receive Jesus Christ's promise and willingly commit their lives to him personally and to the Gospel of God. Christians became his disciples, his followers, his children, his servants, his messengers. We must remain attached, glued as the source of our life, in order to bear fruits. God the Father is the gardener who takes care of the branches so that we may continuously bear fruits in the garden of the Lord. This is a must read book, it is a blessing to the entire Christians family.

BE HOLY FOR I AM HOLY

will help all the believing Christians to know that God is a Holy God, and he want us to be holy in all the things that we do. The book will help you to practice a holy life from this earth to heaven.

"Woe to me! I cried, I am ruined! For I am a man of unclean lips, and I live among people of unclean lips, and my eyes have seen the King, the Lord Almighty." he was so amaze and he screamed, and he realized that he was a sinner, he confessed, repent and was purified by one of the Seraphs who flew to him a live coal in his hand, which he had taken with tongs from the alter" (Isaiah 6:5-6). Christians must learn and know that God is holy; if they are to experience the manifest presence of the glory of God in their life. When prophet Isaiah saw the glory of God in the temple, he screamed and his life changed completely.

THE MESSENGER AND THE MESSAGE OF GOD —VOLUME I, 2, 1 & 2

In the past, God communicated his Word, his Will through the prophets that he has chosen, qualified and anointed with the power of His Spirit to deliver his message to the King, and to the forefathers in the Old Testament. Jesus Christ called the disciples to follow him in His ministry as God the Father called all the prophets to deliver his message to the people in the Old Testament. Today, God has spoken and revealed himself to us by his Son Jesus Christ in a full complete message that transcends all previous words by God. God hath appointed him the heir of all things; by him God made the worlds, both visible and invisible, things in heaven and things on earth.

PRAYER THE SOURCE OF STRENGTH FOR LIFE —English Edition

Prayer the Source of Strength for Life is a powerful book that will energize your spirit to pray more and more until the prayer is part of your life and until the gate of Heaven is opened and your prayer is answered. Your prayer life will change your life.

LA ORACIÓN FUENTE DE FORTALEZA PARA LA VIDA —Spanish Edition

Dios nos dio el poder de la oracion, quiere que lo usemos; debemos llamar, comunicarnos con el en todo lo que estemos pasando. Él espera saber de nosotros.

SPIRIT POWER VOLUMES I AND II

Spirit Power Volume I and II both discuss the power of the Holy Spirit in the lives of believers. The power of the Spirit of God begins from the creation of the world until today. That power will also continue until Christ returns to reign. Hallelujah.

THE CROSS AND THE CRUCIFIXION

Our Lord Jesus Christ died on the cross to bring forth love and compassion. The impact of sins on human life brings all other evil into our world, from one society to another society, from one culture to another. But in Christ, we are clothed with His holiness. We have the gift of eternal life. The gate of Heaven is open and we are eligible for our inheritance in Heaven. Hallelujah! Hosanna in the Highest. Jesus Christ paid it all, unto Him all we owe. The cross of Christ is the cross of joy, peace, and righteousness to all who believe in Him.

THREE SIMPLE SOLUTIONS FOR WORLD PEACE

Three Simple Solutions for World Peace is a book that clears all the confusion that many people of the world have been going through for many years. It is a book that gives light and advice to some of the problems that plague the world, and that offers solutions for these problems. It is a book that is full of knowledge, understanding and solutions that will bring some peace to the world.

JUSTIFICATION BY FAITH ALONE IN CHRIST ALONE

Justification by Faith Alone in Christ Alone will clear all the confusion of believers' faith in Jesus Christ. Believers will also rejoice in the long-sufferings—they will rejoice in their sufferings, afflictions, persecutions, rejections and all various trials that may press in on them because these long-sufferings will help all of the believers to be redeemed in Christ.

CHRISTIAN CELL PHONE SERIES

Christian Cell Phone Godly Wisdom helps readers understand the role of God's wisdom and the importance of obtaining godly wisdom in one's life to produce prosperous results in all areas of life. These areas are critical and include family, relationships and finances. The acquiring of God's wisdom is to be sought after in life and will affect others as well.

Christian Cell Phone God's Favor is designed to give readers knowledge of God's favor from the Old Testament to the New Testament. With an analysis of the favor that was on Jesus, the Son of God, the reader will find that God's favor can completely change one's life and lead others to Christ as well.

Christian Cell Phone God's Anointing is an examination of the anointing on the life of Jesus that includes present day believers in Christ Jesus. This anointing can be applied to all areas of life and can be seen in miraculous ways. The anointing is what makes our life incredible and supernatural, drawing all of those who see, to Christ.

JESUS CHRIST THE JOY OF CHRISTMAS

Jesus Christ the Joy of Christmas gives praise and tribute to the child who was born in Bethlehem. Tracing the prophecies of Old about this King that was born, the author gives an account of the sinless Lamb of God who came to take away the peoples' sins from a biblical perspective, who is the real Joy of Christmas.

PRAYER FOR THE BULLY VICTIMS AND THE BULLY TOO!

Prayer for the Bully Victims and the Bully Too addresses the issue of the bully from the classroom to the home. By the use of scriptural application, the author looks at what can be done to help the bully kid and their victims. The author has written several key prayers that readers can use to help either the bully victim or parents who are dealing with a child who has become a bully.

I AM THE RESURRECTION AND THE LIFE

I Am The Resurrection and The Life: Powerful, inspirational and written from a firm biblical perspective, multipublished author Grace Dola Balogun, gives life to others through the power of Jesus Christ who is the resurrection and the life. This book will open eyes to the amazing and abundant blessings of accepting Jesus Christ as your Lord and Savior, giving keen insight into the Scriptures on the power available to all through the Holy Spirit with an emphasis on aspects of eternal life for the believer.

I AM THE ETERNAL LIFE

I Am The Eternal Life: Encouraging, uplifting and filled with a sound biblical perspective, this book encourages believers and non-believers alike to look to the One that is Jesus Christ, the Son of God, who is the bread of life and the one who gives eternal life to all who believe in Him. This book gives readers a heavenly perspective on their life, revealing believer's God-given destiny and purpose to all who call on Jesus Christ as their Lord and Savior. The truth of the Gospel and the Good News is eloquently displayed in this delightful and insightful read.

HE WHO BELIEVES IN ME SHALL NEVER DIE

He Who Believes In Me Shall Never Die is a fascinating teaching, revealing Jesus as the way, the truth and the life—the everlasting life. All who believe in Him shall never die. Beginning from the Old Testament, the author looks at the fall of humanity through the sin of disobedience through Adam and Eve. Comparing this fall to the sin of disobedience today, the author reveals scriptural truths in the lives of Enoch, Elijah and Moses. The author gives insight into the baptism of the Holy Spirit and gives examples of the Spirit's power and the purpose for which the power is given to believers. The author has given key scriptural insights that all who believe in Jesus Christ will have everlasting life in Him that continues to Heaven.

FORGIVE OUR DEBTS AS WE FORGIVE OUR DEBTORS

Forgive Our Debts As We Forgive Our Debtors speaks of divine forgiveness from the Lord and the Lord's commandment to forgive others, including ourselves. With the Lord's Prayer as a foundation, author Grace D. Balogun, explores from the Old Testament to the New Testament meanings of forgiveness and the consequences of sin. The author gives keen biblical insight into the subject of forgiveness, bringing life-changing healing that is only acquired through the power of forgiveness.

SHE MUST BE SILENT: THE GREAT COMMISSION BESTOWED ON BOTH MEN AND WOMEN

She must be Silent: The Great Commission Bestowed on Both Men and Women is a controversial book that takes a look at the role of women throughout biblical history and gives key scriptural insight into the role of women from the Old Testament to the New Testament. An encouraging, enlightening read, this book is recommended for women and men who want to understand the role of women from a biblical perspective. This book does an excellent job in giving insight into key roles that women play in God's redemptive plan and sheds light on the empowerment of the Holy Spirit that is given to both men and women by God, who is no respecter of persons.

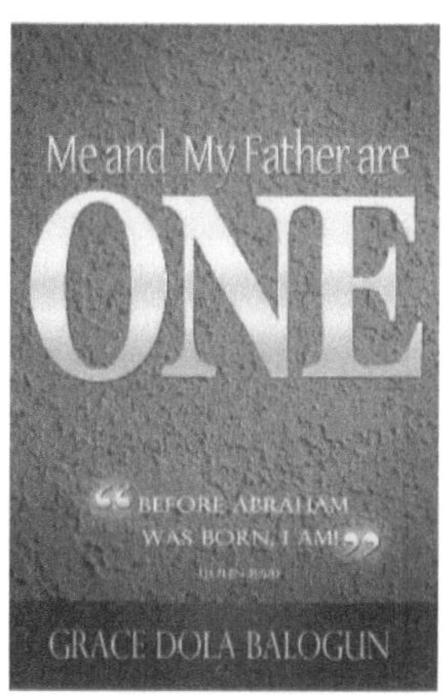

ME AND MY FATHER ARE ONE: BEFORE ABRAHAM WAS BORN, I AM (JOHN 8:58)

Me and My Father Are One: Before Abraham was Born, I Am (John 8:58) explains that God the Father and Jesus Christ are one from the beginning. In this book, the reader will learn that the plan of redemption is from the Father and is carried out through His Son, Jesus Christ, who is the Word of God. In the beginning, before Abraham, before Adam and Eve, Christ says, "I Am." Written from a biblical perspective, the author displays that Jesus Christ was in the beginning and as Scripture says, "He is before all things, and in him all things hold together" (Colossians 1:17).

ABOUT THE AUTHOR

Grace Dola Balogun graduated from Fordham University Graduate School of Religion and Religious Education i n the year 2010 with an M.A. in Religion and Religious Education. She has been a prayer mentor and advisor for many Christians of all denominations for many years.

Visit her online at: www.Gracereligiousbookspublishers.com
Grace's Blog: http://author-grace-dola-balogun.blogspot.com/
Facebook: https://www.facebook.com/grace.d.balogun
Twitter: https://twitter.com/prayersource

To order additional copies of this book, please E-mail:
info@gracereligiousbookspublishers.com.
This book may also be ordered from 30,000 wholesalers, retailers, and booksellers in the U. S., and in Canada and over100 countries globally.

To contact Grace Dola Balogun for an interview or a speaking engagement, please E-mail: info@gracereligiousbookspublishers.com

The Spirit and the bride say,
"Come!" And let the one who hears say,
"Come!" Let the one who is thirsty come;
and let the one who wishes take the free
gift of the water of life (Revelation 22:17).
MARANATHA EVEN SO COME LORD JESUS
(1ST CORINTHIANS 16:22, REVELATION 22:20)

ORDER FORM

TO ORDER YOUR COPY OF ANY BOOK:
NAME:
ADDRESS:
TELEPHONE:
FAX#:
MAIL:
QUANTITY:
MAIL TO:

Grace Religious Books Publishing & Distributors, Inc.
New York
213 Bennett Avenue
New York, NY 10040

Printed in the United States of America

www.ingramcontent.com/pod-product-compliance
Lightning Source LLC
Chambersburg PA
CBHW020557310726
48979CB00008B/1247/J

* 9 7 8 1 9 3 9 4 1 5 5 4 7 *